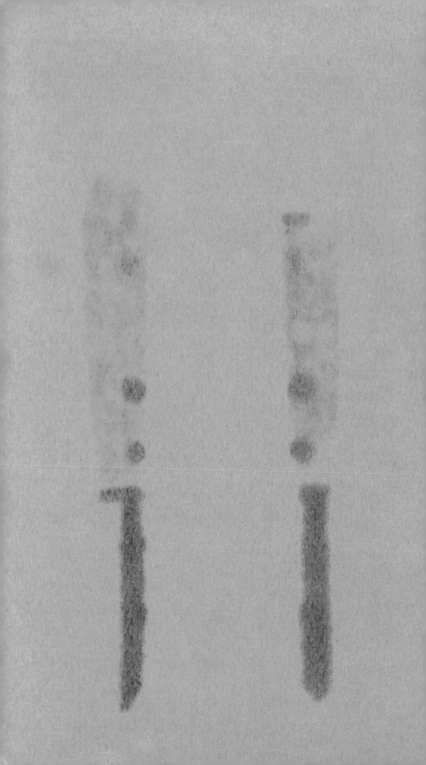

MURPHY'S ROMANCE

ALSO BY MAX SCHOTT

UP WHERE I USED TO LIVE

Harper & Row, Publishers

New York

Cambridge   London
Hagerstown   Mexico City
Philadelphia   São Paulo
San Francisco   Sydney

1817

MURPHY'S ROMANCE

A NOVEL BY

Max Schott

Portions of this book originally appeared in somewhat different form in the Spring & Winter 1977 issues of *Ascent* and in *Up Where I Used to Live,* a collection of short fiction by Max Schott, published in *Illinois Short Fiction* in 1978; they are reprinted with the permission of the University of Illinois Press.

FIRST EDITION

Designer: Gloria Adelson

Drawings: Irving Freeman

Library of Congress Cataloging in Publication Data
Schott, Max, 1935–
  Murphy's romance.
  I. Title.
PZ4.S374Mu [PS3569.C5263] 813'.5'4   79--2657
ISBN 0-06-013781-9

80 81 82 83 84 10 9 8 7 6 5 4 3 2 1

To Julia Demmin and Dan Curley

CONTENTS

PEARBLOSSOM

1965

THERE was a time when I even thought I might try to romance her myself, since everyone else did. But she divined that thought (we were riding horses and my knee sneaked over and rubbed up against hers), and she turned me down. Anyhow, I ended up marrying her aunt.

Toni was friendly as pie after she turned me down (and before, too). I went on keeping my horse out at her place and helped her a little with the horses—she's a horse trainer. In return she kept my horse for me for free. And we got to be pretty good friends. I'd give her advice (still do), which she doesn't mind receiving: just laughs.

One day after I'd known her a couple of years she introduced me to her aunt—that would be four years ago. 'Is your aunt married?' I asked her afterward.

'No, divorced,' Toni said.

'All you women between here and San Diego are divorced,' I said. 'How many husbands has she had?'

'Just one, Murphy, like me. That's enough.'

Well, one wasn't enough for her aunt. We got married three weeks after Toni introduced us. I said to Toni: 'I don't know why you hid her so long.' 'I don't either. I just never thought of it,' she said, 'maybe because she doesn't like horses.'

Turned out Margaret was the next thing to a mother to Toni. All her other relations stopped talking to her years ago, including her own mother and father. If I was her father I think I'd have done the same, but I also have to believe I might have relented when I saw how little good it did.

I remember when I first met her. I'd moved to town from up north and didn't know a soul. The wife I'd had up home had died and been dead two years. So I'd sold out, sold everything and retired to Pearblossom, bought a house, and here I was just sitting on my hands.

Up north, whenever I could get out of the store I'd go out on the desert—lots of big ranches up there—and ride after cattle. I liked it and it kept my blood running; but down here I didn't even have a store to try to get out of. I'd sit in the café and rechew the newspapers, and when I couldn't take any more of that I'd go out and drive my pickup around on these desert roads, which are all straight as strings and numbered A to Z in one direction (running east and west), and 1 to 100 in the other, with

4

every tenth one laid right along the section line; easy to find your way wherever you wanted to go, but I didn't know where that was. After a couple of weeks I began to think, 'Well, if this is heaven I've had enough of it,' and I decided to go out and shop for a horse.

I'd seen plenty of them around. We're only sixty miles from Los Angeles here, and some of the excess money from there finds its way to Pearblossom. Rich people who can afford the electricity bills on these deep wells buy little irrigated farms for themselves and raise horses, or keep one or two to ride or even just to look at.

So I went out shopping. I didn't know what I'd do with a horse if I had one. The few cattle I saw were penned up in small fields. And I didn't feel old enough yet to just ride my horse up and down the road shoulder with the kids. Didn't even have a saddle: before I left up there I took my saddle and bridles down to the weekly sale and had them auctioned off—I was going to retire for sure.

I was driving along 30th Street east just before noon, and when I came to the corner of J, I saw a place, The Buckhorn, and thought I'd stop and eat (no deer on this desert and haven't been for centuries—they name these places just whatever comes into their heads).

I sat down at the counter, waitress came along and asked what I'd like. Nice girl. I know her and her husband both now. 'Just a bowl of soup, please,' I said, 'No! —make it chili—chili with some bread and butter and a piece of that pie: best not regret a meal till after you eat it.'

'All right,' she said, and laughed. (I don't know how such a large proportion of waitresses stay as civil as they do, given the job they have.)

I ordered coffee to drink and when she brought it I

asked her: 'Know where there's any horses for sale?'

'Not really, it's out of my line. But you could look over there on the wall. There's usually some horses. You can put up a notice yourself if you want to. Some horse people come in here.'

'That right? Thanks, maybe I will.'

I did: I looked on the wall and I put up a notice: 'Good well-broke horse wanted—smooth mover,' and my name and phone number. And I saw a business card tacked up: HORSES TRAINED/HORSES BOARDED/HORSES BOUGHT AND SOLD. Toni Wilson.

'Does it all,' I said to myself. Up where I came from women horse trainers weren't too common, and the ones I'd seen were built on the order of Calamity Jane: you'd have to peel them down quite a ways to determine the gender, and you never would be sure of the sex. With a name like Toni I didn't have much hope for an exception, though I won't say I gave it much thought.

Next day, I drove out to her place. No one seemed to be around the barn, and from the dust I found my way out to the arena.

There she was, on horseback, working cattle with a dog to help her and a man perched on the fence looking on (turned out to be the owner of the horse—big long new car parked behind him getting covered with dust). I turned off the motor and sat in my pickup and watched.

She was pretty. Looked like a woman, and sounded like one (first thing I heard her say was 'Oscar'—seemed that was the name of the dog). Appeared to be nothing the matter with her but her name and occupation. She looked about thirty (she was thirty-five and looked it up close); had a scarf tied around her head, which made almost a perfect oval of her face. Her hair was dark brown and she still had her complexion. I don't know why she doesn't tan or blister to pieces working out in the weather like she does—and she won't wear a hat, just that scarf to keep off a little of the dirt her horse and the cattle kick up. If she'd stay in the house she'd be white and rosy red to this day, but even as it is she just takes a little sunburn one day and loses it the next. Must have a good skin cream.

There was a bunch of ten or twelve steers standing at one end of the arena. She'd separate one out from the bunch and make the horse block the steer from getting back with the others where he came from—anyhow that was the object. She could ride all right, but the horse needed more help than he could get just from a rider. He wasn't much, and she'd worked up quite a sweat trying to make him look better than he was. I watched her separate a steer out from the herd, gentle little steer not bent on moving too fast; but he seemed to think he'd like to get back to the herd if it wasn't too much trouble, and he made a little feint in one direction, and while the horse was trying to untangle his feet and get in front of the steer, the steer turned back the other way and trot-ted back to the herd—never drew a deep breath. She brought out another one, even gentler, who just jogged off to the far end of the arena. 'Oscar,' she said, and Oscar jumped out from under the far fence and ran and grabbed the steer by a hindleg and dropped flat on his belly with his chin on the sand, so the steer kicking out at what bit him kicked over the top of Oscar's head. That sent the steer looking for a way past the horse and back to the herd. 'That's enough,' she said, and Oscar ran back and crouched under the fence again and watched her for a fresh instruction. But enough was too much, given that horse. The steer angled across the arena toward the herd at a trot, and she went to head him off. Looked pretty serious about it—swung her little leg five or six times, gouging the horse in the belly with a spur, and managed to get him up to full speed. And when the horse got to a place in front of the steer, the steer stopped, and she stopped the horse—so far so good—blocked him there. But when the steer turned and started up again, for that horse to turn and do the same at the same rate of speed as that steer was just more than nature provided for. So he got away back to the herd.

She laughed—probably didn't feel much like it—and since the horse was breathing hard from the effort of trying to move she walked him over my way to let him catch his breath and see what I might want.

Some of her forelock had fallen out of the scarf and plastered itself to her forehead, which was running sweat. She reached up and tucked it back. I didn't like to see a woman jangling her spine on a horse or sweating like a man (or anyway didn't approve of it), and I don't like the idea even to this day, though I've had to get used to it.

I got out of the truck when I saw her coming, climbed up on the fence and took my hat off.

She aged a little as she got closer—had a vertical groove between her eyes that you couldn't make out at a distance. But I still liked her better up close. Seemed her features weren't quite regular. Her nose isn't straight, though I wouldn't call it crooked. Anyway there's something there that isn't straight: I've looked at her a million times and she looks a little different every time; can't ever seem quite to get a straight, settled look at her, and I'd say that nose is why.

I wasn't sure how to address her. She looked old enough and cheerful enough to have tried marriage at least once (even where I came from); she didn't have a ring on, but horse people sometimes won't wear them, for fear of slicing a finger off in a tangle of some kind.

'Mrs. Wilson?' I said.

She nodded. 'Toni,' she said, and thumped the horse in the side with her heel so that he moved sideways over to the fence. She put her hand out for me to shake.

'Glad to meet you,' I said. 'My name's Murphy Jones. Just dropped by to see if you might happen to have a—'

'You're in the market for a smooth mover,' she said, and laughed. 'I was going to call you. I don't know whether I ever would have; but I saw your note at the café and copied down the number. Glad you came by.'

'I'll be darned,' I said. 'Well, I am. I'm more or less looking for a horse to buy just to ride around on. I can see you're occupied at the moment, though. Is it all right if I just sit and look on?'

'Sure. If you have the time I'll show you what I have soon as I'm done.'

'All the time in the world,' I said.

'Are you from Oregon?' she asked me (she saw the plates on my truck).

'Used to be,' I said. 'Native of Pearblossom now.'

'If I don't have anything that suits you, I can tell you where some are, too,' she said, 'if you don't know your way around yet.'

'That would be fine,' I said. 'I could use some directing.'

So she showed the man his horse, talked to him for a while by the fence, and after he left she rode to the barn and I drove along behind. 'She looks good on a horse, even on that one,' I said to myself. 'A shame though, if she's got to ride, to be seen on a sow's ear like him,' and it crossed my mind (just a passing thought, luckily) that I should buy a good horse and pay her to train it. Seems every time I look at her I want to spend money on her —true to this day. Maybe I'm getting old, or it could be because she's short. Don't know what makes her short either; her legs are long; surprised me when we got up to the barn and I saw her swing off onto the ground from the back of that horse (jeans fit her like a second skin); 'Sure has long legs,' I said to myself; odd thing is, her torso doesn't seem short either, but she's short for all that. Jeans are about all she'll ever wear. Maybe once a year, if I'm lucky, I'll take her by surprise out downtown at night and she'll be wearing a dress: doesn't look half bad in one.

She brought a bay mare out of a stall and put a saddle on her—had her own method of hoisting a saddle up onto a horse's back, like I had when I was a nine-year-old boy. 'That's a pretty mare,' I said, 'but not to waste your time —I've always rode geldings.'

'You have? Why?' she said.

'Nothing personal,' I said. 'Up where I come from we keep our saddle horses all in a bunch, and a mare in amongst them makes the geldings hard to catch; so we never get in the habit of using them.'

"That's no excuse now,' she said.

'No, but I'm used to it now. Just a prejudice I grant you. I don't doubt a mare's almost as good as a horse, if it's a good mare.'

She laughed—though she looked at me a second first to see whether I knew I was making a joke.

'But if you were going to ride her anyway this afternoon, I'd like to watch and see how she moves. I've never seen many women horse trainers.'

'I'll show her to you then,' she said, and she rode her around a little. Nice mare.

Then she brought out a gelding, good-looking three-year-old—just a baby; where I come from we wouldn't think he was old enough to break, but they do everything faster down here. Pretty animal: nice long shoulder, long hip, slim neck, good flat bone in his legs and not a bump or blemish on him. Big bright eyes, not unkind. Too good for what I wanted one for, just to idle around on.

She put a saddle on him and got up on him and walked him off, and he moved just like he looked: put every foot just where she asked him to. She stopped him and laid the rein against his neck and he turned round and round like a turnstile. Then she stopped him and drew in the reins and he tucked his chin and ran backward almost as fast as that first horse I'd seen her on could run ahead.

'Regular prodigy,' I said. 'I sure enjoy seeing you ride him. But I won't even ask you what you want for him. I've got no use for a horse of that caliber. I knew it when you led him out, to tell the truth. How much do you get for a horse like that though, just out of curiosity?'

'Twenty-five hundred dollars, is what I'm asking,' she said.

Well, that made me swallow. 'Doesn't surprise me,' I said. 'Not overpriced either. Sorry to have put you to so much trouble, though.'

'I don't mind that,' she said. 'Anyway, I wanted to improve my image.'

'You can't make ham out of lard,' I said. 'You looked good even on that first one. Kind of a wrastling match though.' 'But imagine a woman who looks like you do

11

worrying about what someone thinks of her horse-training ability,' I said to myself.

She gave me some addresses and said to stop back by and visit when I could. Cordial as could be. I like them to be cordial. Best way to be reminded where you stand. And it's hard to see how I let it slip my mind later on.

I looked at a few horses here and there around town, even went to the auction on Saturday night and bid on a couple. The next week I bought one way out on 60th Street. I called her up afterward and asked her if I could board him at her place.

'Sure, Murphy,' she said.

'About how much would it run me?'

'Forty dollars a month,' she said.

'That sounds all right,' I said (actually it sounded pretty high, coming from where I did, where hay, rent, labor, land and just about everything was cheaper).

Next morning she drove me out to where he was, and we hauled him back to her place in her trailer. She was curious as a jay. Asked me this and that about the town I was from, what I did there, why I left, what kind of horses we used around there, how old they were when we first broke them and what we used in their mouths. And afterward she wouldn't let me pay her for the hauling. Friendly.

I asked her where I could get a saddle made. She told me to try one of hers. If I liked it I could get one made by the same boy, right here in Pearblossom. And whether I did that or not, anyway it would give me something to ride until I bought one.

I went out the next morning to ride my horse, threw one of her saddles on him, and she asked me if I'd like to ride out with her and help get the cattle into the arena from the field.

After that I'd come out every morning to exercise old John, and since she seemed to like it I'd help her a little. I'd ride out with her and Oscar to bring the cattle into the arena from the field, then lead a horse or two out from the barn to the arena and tie them up ready for her to ride. She rode four or five horses every day before noon, which is a lot.

And as a man in the position I was in will (if he doesn't have better sense), I started having daydreams.

I liked the saddle all right, and one day I went into the saddle shop, walked through about an acre of western clothes and found the saddlemaker in a room at the back. Young fellow, like she'd said.

I mentioned her name as the person who recommended him, said I'd been riding one of his saddles, and after I placed an order I said: 'Sure seems to be a fine woman, that Mrs. Wilson.'

'Sure is,' he said.

'If I was a single young man I'd be right after her.'

'I would too,' he said, 'but you don't want to let a thing like that stop you, from what I hear.'

'Why's that?' I said. 'Like what?—had enough of wedded matrimony, has she?'

'Hasn't time for it,' he said. 'Goes through men like popcorn.'

I didn't know how well he knew what he was talking about—could be he spoke from experience. Anyway, I verified that conversation by some others. Seemed she was a fast mover; and I didn't see anyone in pursuit.

One morning, it must have been a Monday, we were riding out across the desert (Toni liked to ride out like that on Mondays to unwind the horses after they'd stood idle in the stalls all the day before). She was riding one and leading another, and I was leading one for her from

John. Oscar loped around in the sagebrush, chasing rabbits that often as not would sit and look at him while he ran in circles trying to find them. When he was working around cattle he moved like a cat and never missed a trick. Out here he made a fool of himself, but I believe he did it half on purpose, which is more than I can say of myself.

I rode over so close to her that one of my knees bumped up against hers before anyone could stop it, and the horses we were leading started to bite each other—which seemed sort of romantic.

I don't know if she'd seen it coming or got her first inkling from the knee itself. She let about a minute and a half pass, during which her mouth got thinner than I'd ever seen it—must have been pressing her lips together coming to a decision, or not to a decision but trying to figure out how to use the decision she'd come to a minute and a half ago.

'Murphy, I want to make you a deal,' she said.

'I want to make you one, too,' I thought.

'Sure, name it,' I said.

'If you can keep helping me like you have been, I'll board John for you.'

Well, I understood the language: seemed she was announcing she wasn't taking gifts, not from me. Kindhearted enough way of turning a man down—and I felt that even at the moment.

'You're already boarding him,' I said.

'You know what I mean. I like the help but I can't keep letting you do it for nothing.'

'I've more money than fleas,' I said.

'But it's not my money,' she said, 'don't argue.' And she stuck out her hand.

'All right,' I said, and shook it. It was even kind of a relief to have it over with.

She didn't want to say yes so she got in ahead of me and said no, and that should have been all there was to it. A person hates to remind himself of such foolishness, but in the middle of the night I woke up, sat right up out of a sound sleep and said to myself, 'Damn her, she turned me down.' (It had got through to my understanding right away but it took a while to reach my vanity.)

I tossed and turned and fell back to sleep, and that should have been all there was to it. But before daylight I got up—couldn't sit still and went for a drive—told myself I was going for a drive around and to get some coffee. Then when I'd drove around in circles for a while, I found myself out not far from her barn and took a sudden notion to stop by there. She didn't live at her barn; she lived in an apartment in town. She wasn't out at the barn yet (it was just getting light), and whether I'd hoped she would be or hoped she wouldn't be is hard to say. 'I'll just stop in here while I'm out this way and make sure my horse has water in his bucket,' I said to myself. 'You can't check on these people too often.'

Horse had plenty of water. 'Goddamn her to hell anyway,' I said to myself, and squirted some more water in the bucket—nothing else to do. He poked his head out over the stall door and I looked at his head and at a halter hanging by the side of the stall, and I thought to myself: 'Best thing of all would be for her to show up here and find John and every sign of me gone, that'll fix her. I'll do myself the favor of getting me out of her sight, since that's what she seems to want so much. Good thing I got here early. I won't even leave a note. I'll call up later in the day and tell her just as friendly and polite: "Toni, for reasons of convenience I decided to move old John to a stables a little closer to town." Let her try to think of an answer to that.'

I took John out from the stall, grabbed my bridle and saddle blankets, got in my pickup with the lead rope strung through the window and drove out the lane and down the paved road with him trotting alongside. I was going west; she'd be coming to work from the east; I'd just about given up hope when I saw her coming in the mirror. 'Damn it,' I said.

She passed her lane and drove up beside me and waved. I waved good morning to her and just kept going. She pulled past me and stopped, and I waved and went by her, and she passed me up again and turned around and stopped in the middle of the road. There was room for me to go by, but what could a man do but stop?

'Morning,' I said.

'Where are you going?'

'Down this way a mile or two.'

'What for?'

'Place down here I'm going to keep my horse.' We were talking through the drivers' windows and he was standing in the space between our two vehicles; the space wasn't much wider than he was, and he kept waving his ears back and forth like a jackass and rolling his eyes. Didn't know what to make of it all.

'What for?' she said.

'No particular reason. Little closer to town.'

'I think you're being silly,' she said.

'I'm never silly,' I said.

'What about our deal?'

'There are plenty of people who will make the same deal with you,' I said.

'Give me this,' she said, and put her hand on the lead rope up higher than where I was holding it.

'What do you want with that?' I said. But she pulled it and darned if I didn't let her take it away from me. She started back to the barn with him trotting beside her car.

I drove off in the opposite direction, intending to go I didn't know where. But when I got to the next corner I slowed down and said to myself, 'Don't be a bigger fool than you are,' and turned around and went back to the barn. She'd already put him in a stall and was outside by the tackroom, brushing off another one.

'Deal still on?' I said.

'Sure it is,' she said.

'I think I better apologize for all that,' I said. 'I got my feelings hurt and tried to blame you for it—nobody's fault but my own.'

'Oh, that's all right,' she said. 'I'm glad you changed your mind.'

'Had to, to get my horse back,' I said.

*   *   *

After I began to be acquainted around town I bought the Pearblossom Livestock Auctionyards, which made me pretty busy in my own right, and I naturally moved John over there.

I hold a horse sale every Friday night. Toni would buy a horse through my sale now and then; I'd even warn her off some of them; and if I ran onto someone who wanted a bit of training done I'd send them to her. We'd see each other at the sale and here and there around town and sometimes I'd drop by her barn; usually we had a horse trade or something to talk about.

Once in a while I'd take her to lunch; still do. I'll try to take her, but she won't let me pay. I said to her one day: 'Look, I've got money and you don't, so why don't you let me buy?—won't hurt you and it will make me feel good.' But she just stuffed a bill in my pocket and I had to humor her.

Another time I asked her: 'Toni—tell me what you see in these polliwogs? That fellow Margaret and I saw you with night before last, his face isn't even formed yet.'

'You'd be surprised, Murphy.'

'That's no answer,' I said. 'I've been surprised for a long time. But since the subject happened to come up, one thing I want to ask you: you're an intelligent woman—and yet you take so little thought for the future. I don't understand it.'

'What do you mean?'

'Well, you rent that apartment from month to month. You work hard and don't save anything, and that's a dangerous business you're in. Don't you ever worry?'

"They won't insure me.'

'I know they won't and I don't blame them. And you're not a bad-looking woman as women go, so—'

'So why don't I marry and settle down before it's too late? Who do you recommend?'

'Almost anyone,' I said, 'if he's a good solid man your own age and with a decent job. You've got to like him, too, with your disposition, or else you'll just make a mess of it.'

'But who?'

'How am I supposed to know who?' I said. 'But you ought to be thinking about it.'

'Oh, it crosses my mind, don't worry.'

Couldn't make a dent. I talked to Margaret about it.

Not long after we married I said to her: 'You know, that Toni's gate swings pretty fast—that's what everyone says.'

'Oh, I know what they say,' Margaret said.

'Well, they say it for a reason,' I said. 'I may be the only man she's ever turned down.'

'Foolish of her,' Margaret said, 'but I don't mind what she does.'

'I suppose there's no use advising her?' I said.

'There isn't,' she said, 'but I don't have any advice to give anyway.'

'You don't live the way she does.'

'Well, I'm old.'

'I'll bet you never did.'

'No, but who does she harm?'

'Herself,' I said. 'If she had money and the fountain of youth, that would be one thing, let her play. Take yourself; you have a job, you're on a retirement plan, you have disability insurance, you married me—you've looked out for yourself.'

'Oh, I don't care about most of that,' she said.

'You do, you care about it or you wouldn't have it. You may not care *too* much about it—you don't have to because you took care *of* it—and if you didn't you'd be a fool!'

'Well, I wouldn't want that,' she said.

'Even if you'd never met me and never remarried, you've provided for yourself.'

She smiled.

'Yes, I know I said something stupid!' I said.

Then, about a year later, we were having pretty much the same conversation when Margaret said to me: 'We could give Toni some of your money.'

19

'We could,' I said, 'I wouldn't mind. But if I saw one of her nighttime companions spending my money downtown I'd cut my throat on the spot.'

'I wouldn't want that,' Margaret said. 'But we'll be dead when she needs it most, chances are.'

So we did, we settled some money on her in a will, fifteen thousand dollars. But that won't change anything and I told Margaret so. 'And even if it would, I still hate to see a person like her carry on like she does, with no thought for the future.'

'Well, that's closer to the truth,' Margaret said. 'But I don't see what you can do about it.'

And so she went on, Toni did, went on in the same way with very few words of advice from me.

Then here not long ago—she was forty years old exactly—a horse fell over on top of her and put her in the hospital. I had the luck to be there and see it. Knocked her so cold that for the first half hour she slept like a baby.

For a couple of days she was half unconscious; the third morning she was better. Weak as a cat and sore (she'd broken some ribs), but clear-headed.

I was heading through the hospital lobby that morning to see her when I met the man of the week, Lyle, coming out. 'How is she?' I asked him.

'You have a minute?' he said.

'Sure. How's she getting along?'

'She's all right, I guess,' he said.

'Let's sit down,' I said. We sat down on the edges of a couple of overstuffed chairs there in the lobby and leaned toward each other. I don't like to talk to him standing up. This Lyle could pass for Hercules: must weigh two hundred and twenty or thirty pounds and not an ounce of fat on him. He doesn't look too tall till you get right up to him, but I'm five feet ten and my neck gets sore talking to the man for any length of time.

I used to wonder what he and Toni found to talk about between rounds, since he didn't know a thing about horses; but at least he was a grown man and all of thirty-five years old.

'She's in there crying now,' he said, and wiped his forehead with the back of his hand.

'Crying? What about?'

'I don't know any more about it than you do,' he said. 'When I went in I sat down beside her and said hello and she just stared at me, so I put my hand on her shoulder and said, "Toni?—Hi." I guess that was the wrong thing . . . but how could that be the wrong thing?'

'Couldn't be,' I said.

' "You look better," I told her, and she said, "I don't want to see you anymore," that's all she said.'

'That's a shame, Lyle,' I said. 'Had you been having your troubles?'

He shook his head. Poor guy. His eyes started to fill. If she'd pulled a mallet out from under the sheet and thumped him one on the forehead the big ox couldn't have been more surprised. Dressed up like I'd never seen him, too (I used to see him mostly on his noon hour; he works construction jobs and they say he's useless as teats on a boar). All dressed up and full of sympathy and good feeling and gets the boot.

I reached up past his knee and patted him on the shoulder. 'Nothing more you could have done, Lyle,' I said. 'And what was said after that?'

'Nothing.'

'Didn't you say anything?'

'She rolled over far as those tubes would let her and

turned her head away. I kept putting my hand on her shoulder and on her head and I'd pet her and say her name and she'd just twitch me off like a fly. So I left. Because I was ashamed to sit there anymore because it seemed like she would have got up and left if she could, just to get away from me. And she wouldn't say anything, she wouldn't even tell me to go away. I didn't know what to do so I said "Goodbye" and left. You think I should have left?'

'I'd say you did right,' I said. 'She's not herself, chances are, Lyle. Tomorrow let's hope she'll be taking it all back.'

But tomorrow she didn't. I don't know what was said at the next interview, if she granted him one, but that was the end of Lyle.

I walked down the hall to her room and looked around the edge of the door (it was a three-bed room but she was in there alone). 'He wasn't kidding,' I said to myself. She was turned over as far as she could toward the wall and sobbing away so that her shoulders shook, which must have hurt with those broken ribs.

A couple of hours later I called her up.

'Toni? How do you feel?' I said.

'Murphy? Oh, I don't know, I'm better but I don't feel very good.'

'What's wrong?'

'Just low. I'm all right. Are you coming in?'

'If you'd like me to, sure. I was figuring on it.'

'Okay.'

'If you're not in the mood I can come later on in the day.'

'No, that's all right. I'm not in the mood for anything else, either,' and she laughed, wasn't a very good-humored-sounding laugh and went well with the joke. Didn't sound like her.

So I picked up her mail—three days' worth—and went back to the hospital.

This time she was sitting up. I looked at her and forgot about the way she'd sounded. The day before she'd looked to be a person who was sure enough sick: groggy (they'd had her doped up) and pasty and drawn. But today she looked like the star of the movie playing sick. Took me by surprise. She'd brushed out her hair (which was almost always tied up in some kind of knot or under a scarf when I'd see it), and her face was pale and just a little wan. She looked pretty and soft and at the mercy of things—in a hospital bed and without her clothes or her ordinary ways—a regular candy bar. 'You look a lot better,' I said.

'I feel better,' she said, and smiled a little smile—which you'd think would be a good sign. Truth was, she may have felt better physically, but she didn't feel like she looked (or I couldn't look close enough to see how she felt —too much of the female showing). She was brittle as glass.

I handed her her mail. 'Thanks,' she said, and smiled another little well-meant smile, one of those where just the lips move and only at the corners.

She started to shuffle through her mail: all bills, ads and magazines. But she was looking for something; she found it, a horse magazine, and started to page through, looking for something again. 'I'm supposed to have an ad in here,' she said.

'Oh, yeah, I remember,' I said.

'Here it is.'

'How'd it come out? Let's see.'

'Wait,' she said, and kept on looking at it like she wanted to eat it.

The biggest part of the ad was a photograph and I knew what it was before I saw it. Same old picture she always advertised her training business with: taken years ago of a mare she had a sentimental attachment to, the one that started her in the business and the first one she'd trained (retired now, raising colts and almost too old even for that). In the picture the mare was up on her toes in front of a yearling steer that was making a rush for the herd. She had her knees bent out like a daddy longlegs and her head down almost on the ground so she could block the rush and look the steer right in the face. The picture was a good one and old Desert Lass had been a good mare, and Toni was eager to look at the picture everytime it got printed. But usually she was more discreet about it.

When she finally let me see the magazine I saw she'd only bought a sixteenth of a page, and they'd printed the ad in the upper-right-hand corner of the right-hand page, where a lot of people would cover it with their thumbs and never notice it. 'So she's the one that put you in the business!' I said. 'Came out all right.'

She didn't answer right away, and when I looked up she was looking at me with big round eyes. They're brown, don't know if I ever mentioned it. 'Do you think very much about dying?' she said.

'Dying? . . . well, I keep it in mind sort of as a possibility.'

'If you knew how I feel you wouldn't joke.'

'I guess I don't know how you feel. You haven't told me. Better tell me.'

'Lonely.'

24

'You have friends. You know you're not going to die from those broken ribs.'

'None of that has anything to do with it.' She gave her head a shake, half as if she was angry, and shifted her knees. I saw the shape of a fair amount of flesh shifting under that hospital gown. 'You're quite a ways from dying,' I thought to myself. But there was no way to say so to her.

'Is that why you ran Lyle off? I happened to talk to him.'

'Why?'

'Why what?'

'Why do you think I wanted him to go away?'

'I don't know; that's what I'm trying to ask.'

'I don't know either,' she said.

'I meant: you were thinking you're going to die alone, and he's going to die alone; so you're alone; so you ran him off?'

'I don't know,' she said, and started to laugh (she could laugh but I wasn't allowed to joke).

'What's so funny?' I said.

'I tried to think about Lyle lying awake nights thinking about dying.'

'He's human, isn't he?'

'I don't know. Maybe,' she said, and laughed and wiped her eyes. 'Oh, it hurts,' she said.

'You'd better stop it then.'

'Are you mad at me, Murphy?'

'Your feelings are rushing around and I don't understand everything you say—so it makes me nervous. But that's all right. I'm not mad at you.'

'You were here and saw Lyle?'

'Saw you, too. You were crying so I didn't stay.'

'Is today the tenth?'

'That's right. Thursday. Why?'

'Bills.'

'Oh, don't open those. Leave them lie. I should have sorted them out and left them at your place.'

'I want to open them,' she said. She opened several. Once she laughed, once she said, 'What's this? I thought I paid that. Oh, I remember.' Nothing out of the ordinary, only all in a high-pitched voice. Then she opened another no different from the rest, looked at it and started to snuffle, which was a relief. 'I don't know what's the matter with me,' she said.

'You're not alone,' I thought, and it crossed my mind as a hope that she might run me out.

'I think I'll be all right now,' she said. 'You can leave if you want to.'

'I don't want to.'

She made a motion to push her mail away, and I got up and took it away from her; quick as it was off her lap her lower lip started to quiver, turned down, and she really cut loose.

'There, there,' I said, and after what seemed the longest time she began to slow down. 'I'll tell you what: I'll sort these out and make out the checks and the envelopes. If you're short, Margaret and I will make you a loan. Margaret suggested it yesterday, but to tell the truth we thought you'd be lying here dreaming in Technicolor for a few days without a worry in the world, or we'd have mentioned it sooner. All you have to do is tell me where your checkbook is. Is it home? On your table?'

She nodded, so I kept talking.

I told her she'd see it all in a new light in a day or two, talked about shock and what a session she'd had with that horse and in the hospital, and how with all that sugar water and leftover morphine in her veins it was no wonder she felt like she did. Since she was making me say it neither one of us believed a word of it, maybe; but she had her cry and was the calmer for that. She'd worn herself out, and by the time I got to the end of what I could think of to say she could hardly keep awake.

She apologized and said she really would be all right now and just felt sleepy. I asked her if she'd like Margaret to come in and see her later on.

'I'd like that a lot,' she said, and nodded and gave me one more of those little smiles, which I was glad to get.

I went home; no one was there, and I started going through Toni's bills.

'What are you doing?' Margaret said when she came in.

'Paying your friend's bills.'

'Toni's? With her money, I hope.'

'No, yours. And I'm about out of patience with her and her bills both.'

'Well, you don't have much.'

'You won't have much either after you see her. You'd better take some Kleenex. If she carries on with me another time or two like she did this morning she'll be looking for someone else to pay her bills for her. I never thought I'd see the day she'd act like that.'

'What did she do?'

'Oh, crying over her bills—which are something to cry over; saying she's going to die—all sorts of nonsense. About half hysterical. I told her she couldn't die of a broken rib, and she says that has nothing to do with it. Seems she's going to die someday no matter what, and she ran Lyle off because he wouldn't promise to prevent it and even is going to do the same thing himself. If I

27

wasn't the closest thing she has to a father she'd run me off, too.'

'Does she have a fever?'

'Not a thing the matter with her. A little weak and sore is all. And so she has to break down in front of an innocent party.'

'Who?'

So Margaret went in to see her.

'And how did she behave this afternoon?' I said.

'She behaved fine. She surely is unhappy though.'

Toni behaved herself all right after that, but was so sad that she looked almost as old as she felt. It took her a couple of months to get her feet under her again. The doctor told her to walk, and she'd walk from the arena to the barn and back with her jaw clenched so that her cheeks bounced and carrying herself as if she had a glass of water on her head. She'd stand at the fence and watch a boy she'd hired exercise the horses. She didn't want him training them, she said, but just to lope them in circles and keep them legged up. She didn't charge her customers for that, but only for board, and she managed to hang on to her customers until she could work again.

For years past she'd trained nine horses at a time and spent all she made. One or two would usually be out of commission or laid up for some reason, so that meant she had seven or eight to ride a day. She couldn't see changing her ways, yet knew she couldn't go back and do that.

'You're fighting the bridle,' I told her. She said she had to keep going the same way because of the money, and maybe she believed that. But I made her see on paper that she could make as much or more without doing near so much herself. I made her sit down and look at the figures.

I told her half of what she did was just dray work anyway: took no talent at all, and some hammer-headed boy could do it—saddling and unsaddling and exercising horses and walking them dry when they were hot. Since she already had a boy hired who galloped around all day like an orangutan, why not put him on steady? She could take in more horses that way, make more money, use more of her skill, pay the boy, and still have less work to do herself. 'Make it easy on yourself,' I said, 'use your head and you'll be training horses another forty years yet.' I gave her a lot of advice, but at first she wouldn't even smile, just look at me like a kicked dog.

Anyhow, one day she got up on a horse again: sat there like a sack while he packed her around. That boy galloping around in circles didn't help matters.

'Does it hurt?' I said.

'No,' she said.

After she got off she said: 'I don't think I can do it anymore.'

'Don't be silly,' I said. 'You know how weak a person gets just from lying in bed a few days with the flu—and you've been idle six weeks.'

'I know,' she said.

'That accident came just at the time to give your spirits a knock all out of proportion to anything.'

'I know it did. I'm getting old.'

'Sure you are,' I said, 'but that won't kill you very fast of itself.'

'I guess,' she said.

'You're used to being so darned strong—so you don't think there's another way to go about things.' (When that horse flipped over on her, while he was still in the air she squeezed the saddle so hard with her legs that the inside of her thighs from her knees to her crotch turned black and blue. Doctor said he'd never seen anything quite like it: bruises, yes, from a blow, but not produced like that by a person's own exertions.) 'These jugheaded boys can take the rougher edges off these wilder colts for you—no skill in that—it's not what people come to you for—isn't that so?—they want those finer touches. You'll have to change your style a little, is all.'

'You've said all that, Murphy.'

'Have I? Well, I'm saying it again then. Just be glad you're a trainer and not an athlete yourself—where when you begin to slow down the least little bit someone will come along and better you.'

I'd talk, and depending on little variations in her mood she'd either get annoyed because she'd heard it all before and knew it already, or she'd look at me as if she didn't believe a word of it, or sometimes she'd give me a little smile—as if she'd done something bad and was sorry.

One morning I asked her: 'You want to drive over and watch old Jim Farr ride?'

She shrugged. 'If you do,' she said, and smiled.

'Then call your dog and climb up in that pickup,' I said. 'I've seen sheep show more vital spirits than you do. I never thought I'd hate to see a woman try to be agreeable, but you act like your will has turned all to Jello.'

'You're cute when you grumble.'

'Too bad I'm not trying to be.'

We found him out riding the lane not far from his house. He lives on a Thoroughbred farm. They give him a house to stay in and whiskey money, and when they have a decent young horse turned back from the track for lack of speed, they let the old man ride it a while and then they can sell it for a saddle horse or polo pony.

Every morning before his nap he rides two or three and that's a day. He must be eighty-five, and so much whiskey has passed over his old glottis that he talks in a sandpaper whisper and always sounds about to lose what's left of his voice.

She introduced me to him a few years ago; turned out I'd heard of him ever since I was a boy. He comes from the same part of the world I do—came down here for the weather about fifteen years ago.

I've seen some photographs of him—published in a book—taken about 1910 or 12: wearing a pair of boots and big-roweled spurs, angora chaps, a necktie, one of those wide-brimmed high-crowned hats like they still use in western movies. But either he dressed up special for the picture or he's in his second or third childhood now: wears high-topped farmer shoes and a red cap, and always has a clean red bandana around his neck, to protect his throat, though he should be trying to protect the inside not the outside.

I used to hear stories about him when I was young. He went from ranch to ranch and harness-broke their workhorses. Great big five-year-old colts who'd never been touched; he'd mesmerize them with a pair of buggy whips and in half an hour he'd walk right up and put halters on their heads.

They told a lot of stories about him, and probably a lot of lies. They say that when a horse would go to bucking he'd reach down and grab him by the flank and tickle him till he quit: but a person would have to have arms half again as long as his are to do that. (Still, when people begin to lie about another person instead of themselves you know he must have done more than just sit and scratch himself.)

They say he'd ride from one ranch to another to harness-break these workhorses, and on the way he'd break colts to ride. He had a donkey with him, too, which he'd harness those big workhorse colts with—leave them overnight in the corral and the donkey'd drag them to water or to the haypile or wherever he wanted to go— kind of a scientific-minded donkey. So traveling along he'd put his pack on the donkey and tie one saddled colt to the donkey's tail, and let the donkey break him to lead; and he'd ride another colt and tie a third to the tail of the one he rode. When the one he was on would buck the one tied to his tail would get scared and lay back and jerk the bucking one back to earth again (I'd be afraid he'd jerk him flat down on top of me). They say he'd turn out half-gentled colts by the sackful like that, just on his way from one place to another.

He recognized us. Lifted his cap to Toni and seemed willing to sit on his horse and talk—and he talked just like anybody. I mean, you could exchange words with him and he made good sense; but it went kind of slow: when you said something it took him so long to answer or even for his eyes to register that it was more like telegrams sent back and forth than what I call conversation.

'Hear anything from that north country?' he asked me.

'Little now and then. What about yourself?'

'Not much, a little.'

After we got through some more talk about as interesting, I said—wanting to get him to show off a little: 'Can a long-legged outfit like that one there be taught to stop, Jim?'

'Some of them can,' he said. 'You think this warm weather will hold?'

'It's been holding for the five years I've been here, so

I guess it will,' I said. 'Not like that country up there.'

'No, that's right. Up there it'll snow on you.'

Looked like he was just going to go on sitting there till we'd leave. I tried again and this time I winked at him: 'This girl here says these Thoroughbred horses are all right for going straight ahead fast and that's about it.'

'I did not,' she said, and elbowed me in the ribs.

'They say this one can't even do that,' he said and laughed. Reached ahead and picked a little tangle out of the horse's mane.

I was afraid vanity had died out in the old bastard, but after a bit he said, 'Let's see if he'll stop today,' clucked his tongue and took off down the sandy lane between the two fields, picking up speed and rocking back and forth a little in the saddle like a leaf on a branch. He galloped a couple of hundred yards and then the horse sat down in the air like a buckshot dog and slid. But they'd kicked up such a fog of sand we couldn't see much.

They came back running just as hard and Jim sort of fluttering in the saddle (I don't want to labor it, but he was weak: he could no more have broken a blood vessel in those pipestem legs of his than fly). When he came even with us he moved a little forward, made his rein hand steady and said 'Ho.'

When Jim asked him the horse was just coming down on his front legs at the end of a stride, and when he felt the pressure firm up on his mouth and heard the man say 'Ho' he tucked his chin, gathered his hindlegs under him for what ordinarily would have been another stride and sat down in the sand and slid about fifteen feet on his hocks (it's a wonder he didn't burn all the hair off the backs of his legs), his front legs dangling, toes just trailing the ground. Sitting straight up like that he looked almost

33

like a seahorse, and had his neck bowed like one.

Jim let his own chin drop while the horse was sliding and let his neck go slack and his head bob, like he might go to sleep. I think he did it for effect.

The horse stood at the end of his tracks without lifting a leg. The only sign of nervousness was he ground his teeth. Jim looked back at the marks he'd made—looked like ski tracks.

'Well, when you think you'll retire?' I asked him.

'Right after dinner,' he said, and laughed—must have been an old joke. 'No, I been retired fifteen years. How about yourself?'

'Seven for me,' I said. 'Semi-retired before that.'

I believed I'd showed her something. Soon as we left I said: 'If you can do that when you're old and decrepit as that whiskey drinker, you'll feel all right won't you?'

'I don't know how I'll feel,' she said. 'I don't even know how he feels. Anyway, I knew him before you did.'

'Watch out or you'll laugh,' I said.

* * *

I gave her a lot of advice. Didn't help, but she got better. No reason why she shouldn't—nothing wrong with her but those broken ribs, and they'd healed. I remember thinking at the time that she wouldn't learn a damn thing from the accident, and that that was a pity. I couldn't decide whether I thought a harder knock would have done her any more good. The one she got seemed hard enough when it happened.

Just when she'd started feeling fairly good again, a man came along who she hadn't seen for years.

Nice-looking fellow, even yet. Lives way off in some

little Nevada town she exiled him to, years back. Had to come this way on business—that's what he said in the note he wrote her.

When Margaret told me Toni'd got the letter, I said: 'Did she mention the man's name?'

'Wendell,' Margaret said.

'Wendell?—isn't he the one she bought that old Desert Lass mare from about a century ago?'

'Same one,' Margaret said. 'She had a romance with him just after her marriage broke up.'

'So she tells me one thing and you another.'

'Well, they're both true.'

'Doesn't surprise me. Lots of buckets dipped in the well since then; wonder she even remembers him.'

'It would be a wonder if she didn't. She wants us to have him over here to supper so that she won't have to spend an evening alone with him unless she decides to.'

'Doesn't want to see him?'

'She wants to,' Margaret said, 'if she could do it without his seeing her. She's afraid he'll be struck by the change.'

'He'll lie if he is,' I said. 'He won't turn and run.'

Toni came over that night and sat down at the kitchen table with Margaret and me. More color in her cheeks than I'd seen in months and I told her so.

'Old friend of yours coming to town, I hear?' She nodded. 'How long's it been?'

'Eighteen years,' she said, and blushed.

'That's a while. He'll be pleased to see how you've turned out.'

'Thanks. He probably won't recognize me.'

'I hope he's done as well. Have you heard from him over the years?'

'Not for a long time.'

'You're full of curiosity then, I'll bet—only natural.'

'A little,' she said. She looked down and rubbed the rim of her cup with her thumb and looked up at Margaret. Seemed I was preventing a conversation; so before long I excused myself and carried my coffee into the front room and started looking over my day book from the auctionyard.

I could hear them jabbering but I couldn't make it out.

'Shut that door,' I hollered. Someone shut it, and I opened the heater vent beside my chair and heard every word.

' "I don't want to see you anymore," I was going to tell him,' Toni said.

'Over already,' I said to myself, 'Damn, they work fast!' But it turned out they were talking about a man named Ben and hadn't even arrived at Wendell yet. One thing on her mind and she'll talk about another.

'And did you tell him?' Margaret said.

'I was too big of a coward,' Toni said, 'but I sort of told him. He knew anyway, and he was sick of me. He wasn't very hard to get rid of.'

'Is he the one you and Bob separated over?'

'Yes, and bless him for that,' Toni said, 'but then Ben and I split up too, right afterward.'

'What was he like?' Margaret said.

'Ben—I've known a Ben or two myself,' I said to myself.

'Oh, I don't know . . . he wasn't very nice some of the time. He used to sulk about nothing. But he was a cowboy, so I thought he was really romantic. I was only twenty-two. He ran a riding stables in Los Angeles during the war —that's where I met him—while Bob was overseas. He'd just come to the city for the first time a year or two before

36

that, and he was always tipping his hat to women and had a drawl, and he looked sort of like a cigar-store Indian—you know, high cheekbones and an eagle nose.

'He even wanted me to divorce my husband and marry him. I said I would; but then I changed my mind. Who knows what I'd think of him now.'

'How old was he?'

'Thirty-five.'

'And why did you change your mind?'

'I don't know, I felt like I needed to be by myself. Besides, he seemed like an absolute stranger to me sometimes—especially when he was sulking. He'd brood for hours for no obvious reason and not say why. It should have made me mad. Now I think it would, but it just mystified me then. I'd look up at him and see this person who was full of thoughts and feelings I couldn't know anything about, except that they were bad, and who was so much older and so different. Maybe now I'd think he was ridiculous.'

'He wasn't violent, was he?'

'Just with people he didn't know, when he was drunk. No, he was very polite and gentle and when he wasn't brooding he liked to talk—in fact he had manners a lot like Murphy's.'

'Ha—talking about me behind my back,' I said to myself.

'I used to like to watch him do things with his hands, especially if he wasn't thinking about what he was doing. I remember, sometimes he'd be talking to someone, they'd be standing by a horse, and he'd start pulling the fly eggs off the ends of the hairs on the horse's shoulders between his fingernails—like this. Isn't it funny the things you'll remember?'

37

'True love,' I said to myself. 'But it's easier to scrape those eggs off with a knife.'

'I'll never forget the day we split up,' she said. 'I had it all rehearsed. He was already mad when he got to my house, because I'd stood him up and then called and asked him to come over. And for six months I'd been driving him and me and Bob all nuts with my changes of feeling. So now that Bob had moved out Ben must have had hopes that I'd behave myself.

'As soon as he sat down at my kitchen table I knew I was right about what I wanted and that I didn't want to see him anymore. I wasn't used to seeing him in my house, and when he laid his hat on the sideboard I understood that he'd taken it off from politeness, but I *felt* like he was trying to take over and should have kept his hat on in my house. And I knew that if I had crazy thoughts like that, I didn't want him there. We'd made all these plans and promises about what would happen after Bob left—in certain moods we'd talk like that, but now it just seemed to me that my husband—or the idea that I had one—had kept the men out of my house and now I had to do it myself.

'He wouldn't drink any coffee, and I just sat there and hung my head and shook it and tried to make myself look pathetic. But he was entirely out of patience. He said, "Okay—what's wrong?—Did you change your mind?" and I remember saying to myself, "Just say *yes,* say *yes,*" and it would have been so easy, compared to the little speech I had rehearsed. But I couldn't.

' "I think I just need to be alone for a few days," I told him.

' "That's easy to fix," he said and got up and put on his hat.

'I said no, it wasn't like that. I loved him but I felt confused and needed a little time. I had to be alone to think things over. I used to tell him the same thing every time my husband would write from overseas, which luckily wasn't very often.

' "Fine, be alone," he said, with that face like a brick. I really wanted to grab him and hug him and break him down—but he looked so angry.

'I made him promise to call me. You know what I think I liked most about him: he was a *grownup* and had a whole set of habits and ways of doing things—even if I didn't like some of the ways. I remember watching him walk off down the driveway: even though he was mad and you could see it in his back, he still walked exactly like himself. He took long steps and never quite straightened his knees, and he never walked fast or slow. He used to measure out postholes to the inch just by walking. Seeing him go made me feel awful. I had a premonition he wouldn't be back, at the same time that I was too stupid to really understand that he wouldn't.'

'Didn't he call?'

'I think he did, once. I asked him to call on Wednesday night—and when it rang that night I wouldn't answer it. I saw him once after that, about a year later—and you know he'd hardly speak! If I saw him this minute he probably'd still be mad. Isn't that ridiculous? Why should anyone act like that? I'm still mad at him, too, but I wouldn't act like that.'

'He got under your skin, I'll say that for him,' Margaret said.

'I guess he did; but I haven't thought about it for years.

'So after that I couldn't go up to Ben's stables anymore and ride his horses. And after about a month of stewing

I decided to buy a horse of my own. That's when I met Wendell. I bought Lass from him and took a few horse-training lessons, and I had a real wild affair with him—the first one like that I ever had, where there wasn't a lot of dawdling around. A good thing there wasn't because the whole thing only lasted two weeks. He decided to go back to his wife, not because of me but because of the judge. When I met him they were separated, and he said they were going to get a divorce. But when the judge told him how much he'd have to pay, he decided to go back.'

'Oh, Toni, you don't believe that, do you? Still?' I heard Margaret say.

'Well, not that that's why he went back; but I believe the judge had a lot to do with the timing. If the hearing hadn't been right then, he wouldn't have gone back right then. Maybe we'd have run through each other, or who knows what might have happened, I don't know. We were both only twenty-two. Anyway, the way it was it was cut off.'

'What attracted you so about him?'

'Well, he was big and tall and strong and handsome—and I'd been sitting in my house for a month. It was lust at first sight.'

'At first sight?' Margaret said.

'Well, if it wasn't I wanted it to be. I wanted to have an adventure.'

'I don't know about that man Wendell,' I said to Margaret later. 'Going back to your wife just to keep money in your pocket—that's a new one.'

'That's not all of it,' Margaret said.

'I'll bet it isn't,' I said. 'but it's all I heard because someone closed that heater vent in the kitchen.'

'I know they did,' she said. 'But I'll tell you some of it. His wife wouldn't let him in the house because he'd been with Toni—and he asked Toni to call her and plead his case for him—can you imagine!'

'Did she turn him down?'

'Yes, but it seems to have been just because she didn't know what to say. He took advantage of all her good feelings. He told her she was too big a temptation for him to resist. So she located him a job and loaned him the money to move. I said to Toni that he sounded a little sneaky to me. Maybe I shouldn't have.'

'Did he pay back the money?'

'Yes.'

'Well, maybe he's all right. He was no more than a kid himself.'

When he came to town Toni called me up to say so. I stopped by her barn to meet him, and I don't know if it's to my credit, but the man did make a good first impression on me.

I found them out in the pasture, standing looking at Desert Lass, who had her head down grazing. Wendell was curly-headed and dark-complected. 'That's the kind women like all right,' I said to myself.

Toni introduced us, and I stood and helped them look at the old mare.

'You know her from way back,' I said.

'I'd never have recognized her,' he said.

'A colt or two and they get a little dough-bellied,' I said.

'Last thing a man would think of when he thought of her was belly,' Wendell said. 'Moved like a cat.'

'A streamlined one will end up more womb-sprung than one who's on the big-bellied side to begin with,' I said.

'Stands to reason,' he said. 'Not much room in there for a colt.'

'That's right,' I said. 'Colt has to bang out a nest for himself and the next one will stretch it on out some more.'

'Must be so,' he said, 'from the looks of her.'

'Agreeable fellow,' I said to myself, 'man you can talk to.'

'How many's she had, Toni?' he said.

'Six,' Toni said.

'My wife had seven, but one died.'

Toni just looked at him.

'That's too bad,' I said. 'Where is it you're from, exactly?'

'Gerlach,' he said. 'Nevada.'

'I know the town but I can't place it. Where is that near?'

'Not too near anywhere,' he said. 'Seventy miles from Fernley.'

'Fernley: I've been through there for sure. Fair-sized place, is it?'

'Fernley? About five hundred in the summer. Right on the paved road, sixty miles west of Fallon.'

'Fallon: I know that place for a fact. Ate supper there and lost a game of blackjack. Hundred miles east of Reno?'

'That's right. You're up that way again, stop by. All good roads. Dirt from Fernley to Gerlach, but it's good ground and you don't even know you're in a car.'

'I will,' I said. 'Train horses up there, do you?'

'Those boys up there don't care if their horses go crooked or in a straight line, and if they don't I don't.'

'I don't blame you a bit,' I said.

'I watch over some cattle for a man. Eight hundred mother cows.'

'That's a lot. Have some men working under you?'

'No, sir,' he said. 'No help but two dogs.'

'Don't see how you do it,' I said.

'I can press my wife into service if I have to,' he said.

'Press her into service?' Toni said.

'If I have to,' he said.

'Been there long?' I said.

'Gerlach?—Ever since I left Los Angeles.'

'You don't strike me like a Los Angeles man.'

'How old's old Lass there, Toni?' he said.

'Twenty-three.'

'Five when I left. Maybe I've changed some.'

'Must be quite a change,' I said, 'to go away off to a place like Gerlach from the city.'

'I don't live right in downtown Gerlach,' he said. 'About thirty-five miles out.'

'How'd you happen to locate there?'

'This old girl right here saw an ad: "Cowboy wanted. High desert. School bus service, house, meat and milk furnished." (They meant a milk cow.) "Two hundred dollars a month. Northern Nevada. Apply Box XXX Western Livestock Journal." Remember that?'

'I remember,' Toni said. 'He wasn't a city person to start with, Murphy. He was pretty much like he is now, come to think of it.'

'I believe it,' I said, 'but they say a person can get spoiled fast, living in town, young country boy especially. Milking that same old cow day in and day out by lantern light might look a little humdrum after your city.'

'Jan milks,' he said. 'My wife.'

'How's she getting along?' Toni said.

43

'Just right,' he said. 'Looks good, feels good—for a woman who's shelled out kids like she has and been alive as long, she gets by all right: that's what everyone says that sees her. I don't pay a whole lot of attention myself.'

'That's too bad,' Toni said. 'I'm glad she's well.'

'She does all right,' Wendell said. 'But you, now, you never settled. I thought you might. Once in a while I'd catch a thought floating through that you'd married and settled down—but you never.' He turned to me. 'Don't you think a person ought to settle down, time you're our age? I understand you're a married man.'

'Darned right,' I said. 'I've been telling her so for years. Just like talking to a log.'

'It takes one to know one, Murphy—a log I mean,' and she gave me a little push on the shoulder.

'I hadn't seen her for a long time, but she looks fine,' he said. 'First thing I said to myself when I saw her: "She looks fine!" Don't you!' and he put his hand on her shoulder and shook her, and I saw her stiffen.

'Yep, I'd have known her on the street anywhere,' he said and put his hand back by his side.

Wendell went downtown to get a room for the night.

When I came home from the auctionyard Toni and Margaret were busy talking in the kitchen. Usually if they're like that and I come in, they'll look at me and start to wink and whistle. But this time soon as she saw me she said: 'I'm sorry, Murphy, if I'd known what he was like I'd never have imposed him on you and Margaret—or on myself.'

'What's he like?' I said. 'Seems to be a nice enough fellow from what I saw.'

'*Uk,*' she said.

'Oh, she exaggerates—unless he's done something?'

'He hasn't done anything,' Toni said.

'He's a good guy,' I said to Margaret. 'Takes care of eight hundred cows almost by himself.'

'He must be all right then,' Margaret said.

'Lives up not too far from where I used to,' I said.

'He's a jerk, Murphy. He has eight hundred and one cows.'

'Eight hundred and a wife and two dogs,' I said, 'but the cows aren't his, they belong to his boss. Didn't I hear you say he's just like he always was?'

'He sort of is,' she said. 'It's hard to explain.'

'And you used to like him. Have you changed so much?'

'I don't think so. I hope not. He used to be very good-looking, I know I'm not wrong about that.'

'Good-looking man right today,' I said. 'You know, I believe she's still carrying a torch.'

'Yeah, fat chance,' Toni said. 'People don't get stupider, do they? I must have had rocks in my head. Poor Jan!'

'My, my, and I have to feed him supper,' Margaret said.

'Oh, he's just an ordinary fellow,' I said. 'Hasn't as much respect for the sex as Toni would like—but I blame his wife for that.'

'What's she supposed to do—punch him in the eye?' Toni said.

He knocked on the door.

'Shall I let him in?' Margaret said.

'Do we have to?' Toni said. 'Let's not!' Then darned if she didn't clap her hand over her mouth and start to have a fit of schoolgirl giggling.

'Too bad we don't have any arsenic,' Margaret said.

'Phaa!' I whispered. 'Now you two behave yourself!

Where do you think you're going?' I said to Toni.

'The bathroom.'

'Act your age, you!'

'Really, Murphy, I have to stop laughing, I'll be back.'

'You're as bad as she is,' I said to Margaret. 'Get out of the way. I'll let him in. Go cook.'

I opened the door. He'd shaved and had his hat in his hands. 'Poor guy,' I thought. 'Come in, come in,' I said, 'good to see you so soon again.' I shook hands with him. 'Come on in the kitchen and meet my wife.'

'Hello,' he said to Margaret. 'Smells good. Toni here yet?'

'In the bathroom doing some last-minute landscaping,' I said.

'Is she?' he said. 'Suits me the way she is. Older than she used to be, but looks fine.'

'You bet,' I said. 'She'll probably ruin it.'

I took him into the front room, and pretty soon she came out, which I was glad to see, and offered him and me some of my whiskey. I'm famous for not being much of a drinker, but I took a drink.

He took one, too, and his flowed straight to his extremities, if I'm not mistaken. Toni was in and out from the kitchen setting the table, and he couldn't keep his eyes off her. He kept trying to get her to look at him, and she kept trying not to—and I believe she had more success.

When she was in the kitchen I said to him: 'I looked at a map a while ago, Wendell, and you know, it wouldn't be a hundred miles from where you live over to where I used to live—if there was a way to get there.'

'Where you from?' he said.

'Little town of Wagontire over in Oregon,' I said. 'Sixty miles north of Likely.'

'Uh huh,' he said. 'Can't place it. Good smell coming out of there.'

'I'll show you on the map,' I said. So I brought out a map, though I had a little trouble getting him to look at it. Toni came out of the kitchen and looked over my shoulder.

'Wendell and I were almost neighbors,' I said. 'Only a hundred miles from my place to his—no roads though—lava rock so thick you can't even ride a horse across. But it's the same country. My old neighbor Sterling Green, he had cattle on both sides.' He sat up at the name. 'Know him?'

'Know him?—damn him! I work for him.'

'Hah!—you see! Margaret, come in here! You women uht—scuse me' ('attack the man,' I started to say) 'and the man works for my neighbor! Here!' and I put out my hand so he had to shake it again.

'Get Murphy another drink,' Margaret said.

'Don't pay them any mind, Wendell,' I said. 'No wonder you take care of eight hundred cows with just a wife and a pair of dogs. He's the shortest-handedest man in the world, that Sterling, damned if he's not!'

Toni went back in the kitchen with Margaret, and I told Wendell a story or two about Sterling. No one could fault me for not being able to talk to a stranger. He didn't have to say a word or even listen.

'That's turned into quite a looking woman, that Toni,' he said. 'Different from what she was, but they say we most of us change a little. Took me a while to get used to it, but she looks better every time she lifts a leg. It's a wonder no one ever married her.'

'She says you're just like you used to be,' I said.

'I've had people tell me I haven't changed; one other

old girl told me I didn't look a day older than I did twenty years ago. I told her, "You don't either," but I lied to her face.'

'I don't blame you,' I said.

'I never pay them much mind,' he said, 'but if Toni says I haven't changed, that's good, the way I see it, because she liked me the way I was; and so to reason it on out, that means there's hope.'

'Just between you and me, Wendell,' I said, 'there's no hope. If I understood you correctly, there's not a hope in the world in that direction. For many another man and boy, maybe, but not for you and me.'

He'd been watching the kitchen door in case she'd run by, but he turned and looked at me like I'd said something in Greek.

We sat down to eat. Toni told us where to sit, and she put herself across at an angle from Wendell, which with only four of us was as far away as she could get; still it was close as he'd got so far, so he proceeded to try to talk to her.

'How's business, Toni?' he said. 'How're the ponies treating you?'

'Fine,' she said.

'You say you had some kind of accident?'

'I'm almost all right now,' she said.

'What happened?'

'A horse fell on me.'

'Now what'd you go and let him do that for?' Wendell said and laughed, big old horse laugh.

'By god, she's right,' I said to myself, 'the man is dense and so was I not to see it.'

'I shouldn't have,' she said.

'I'll say you shouldn't have. I never taught you to do like that, did I?'

'No,' she said. Never cracked a smile. That chilled him a little, but he didn't give it up.

'Training those horses is no business for a woman—don't see why you don't settle down and keep house.'

'She has more than that to keep her from settling down, Wendell. She has oats to sow, so we'd better let her be. Pass Wendell those peas, speaking of oats.'

Margaret and Toni both looked at me, and I was a little surprised myself, when I'd heard what I said. But it didn't faze Wendell.

'What kind of horse fell on you? Just to make conversation,' he said.

'A Quarter Horse stallion; four-year-old,' she said.

'Conversation?' I said to myself. 'If you want conversation so bad, I can give it to you.' 'Shouldn't have been left a stallion but he was,' I said. 'Man that owns him drove all the way to Texas to buy him; but he's a billy goat just the same. I wouldn't breed a mare of mine to him, I'll tell you that, Wendell!'

Wendell turned and nodded at me; thought he could get around me with a nod. 'Never crossed my mind,' he said. 'How'd he happen to fall over on you?' he said to Toni. 'Slip?'

'No,' she said, 'he—'

'Slip ha!' I said (why should I let her trouble herself to talk?). 'He didn't slip, Wendell, I was right there and can vouch for it, you bet he didn't slip!'

'He's really drunk!' Margaret said.

'Phaa—keep quiet,' I said. 'Pass that meat over to where Wendell can reach it.'

'What'd he do?' Wendell said—to me this time—but I wouldn't even look at him.

'Toni,' I said, 'if you'd shown him that stick before you got on him that day—you know the day I mean—I be-

49

lieve he'd never have done it to you.'

'I wish you'd said so at the time.'

'I wish it too, sweetheart.'

'What stick's that?' Wendell said.

'Wendell,' I said, 'you ask about that stick, and I'll tell you: it was a green stick, you see, cut from a bush. About yay long.' I held up my hands. 'At first it was green, but then the sap dried out of it and it shrunk about two inches and turned kind of gray—but it was the same stick and the horse knew it.

'Well, when this horse was first brought to her he had no manners at all. Everytime he saw something alive he'd try to fornicate with it: he'd get up and walk around on his hind legs and beller—you know how they do, Wendell—and his old neck would swell up like a bullfrog's.' Wendell reached up and rubbed his neck, which had swollen and turned pretty red. 'That's right,' I said. 'The horse's manners were right out of Texas. The owner calls him Golden Son of Yellow Moon or something like that, but Toni and I, we always just called him Tex. (Wendell, you just reach over and help yourself.)

'So the first day, soon as he started in to rear and squeal she stepped off and kicked him in the belly a couple of times and cut that stick from a bush. After that whenever he'd begin to titillate himself she'd pound him on top of the neck, right behind his ears: whack-whack-whack. "Cut it out, Tex," she'd say—way you taught her years back, no doubt.'

'Darned right,' Wendell said.

'Darned right,' I said. 'That first day it didn't keep him from carrying on, but by the next day he was sore, and by the time two weeks went by she had his attention, and if his mind happened to start to wander she'd just whisper "Hey now, Tex" in one of his ears. Or if he was sorely tried—say if a mare walked by winking—you know how they'll do, Wendell—with her tail in the air and maybe pissing a little—why Toni'd just hold the stick up where he could see it with his big right eye.'

'Murphy—eat your supper,' Margaret said.

'I don't mind,' Toni said.

'This will interest Wendell,' I said. 'She'd hold it up where he could see it and he'd subdue his old gonads.

'She rode him about six weeks—that was last winter. Then they took him home to breed a few mares with and didn't bring him back till August. And before she got on him that first time again, she found that same little old stick thrown back in a corner of the tackroom. Turned gray, but that horse recognized it, you bet he did, been better if he didn't. But at first she didn't show it to him, just clambered up in the saddle with the stick stuck in her belt, that's the pity of it. Because if he'd had a chance to carry that stick along in his mind's eye, there'd never have been any trouble—that's what I think, maybe a little pawing and squealing, but no trouble.

'He had a good picture of that stick registered in his brain and he hadn't forgot what it was used for—but the memory had slipped way back down into his sub-conscious—that's the way I see it. Wasn't the smartest horse in the world anyway, and darned foolish at times —led astray by his feelings like more beasts than one since the world began—'

'Eat,' Margaret said.

'But I'd hesitate to say to a man that he was outright stupid—just thick-headed. Well, we rode along, came to where there was some mares loose in a field. He looked over the fence at them and must have gone to thinking about the good old days back home, tossed his head and puffed his neck up and nickered at those mares. Rattled your jaw, didn't it, Toni?'

'I don't remember.'

'That's right: I forgot, she doesn't remember a thing. Anyhow, it had slipped Tex's mind that there's a time and place for everything and such a thing in the world as a stick. And to jog his memory she said, "Tex, cut it out," took the stick out from her belt and held it up as of old. He saw it, and it all came back to him, too much all of a sudden, and he threw himself over backwards— landed flat bang on his right side and right on top of her. Darned if I ever saw anything quite like it, Wendell. Looked like he'd been electrocuted.'

'And you don't remember a thing?' Wendell said.

'No,' she said. 'I woke up in the hospital.'

'That was unforgiving ground, too—sand, but packed down. When Tex got up and ran off she never wiggled. Scared me.'

'Aw,' Wendell said, 'I hate to think of you lying there like that.' And he laid his big right arm out on the table like a ham. I don't know if he expected her to reach across and take his hand in hers or butter it or what. 'Sorry I ever got you started training those horses,' he said. 'A woman like you doesn't need to be in a business like that. If I didn't live so far away I'd see to it that you weren't.'

'I hope *you're* drunk, too,' Margaret said.

'Good thing you live so far away,' Toni said. 'Just how would you go about seeing to it?' And she laid down her fork and looked him right in the eye.

'Ha!—Watch out, Wendell, you hound!' I said to myself. 'Wendell—' I said.

'I don't know *how*,' Wendell said, 'but I'd stop you training those horses, because it's only right.'

'Wendell, my friend,' I said, 'I don't know how it is in Nevada but in Pearblossom the cats scratch. If you antagonize them, I mean. Otherwise they won't, I think. So you'll have to bark up another tree, if you can find any.'

'I'll make some coffee,' Margaret said.

Toni covered her mouth with her napkin.

'I didn't catch all that,' Wendell said. 'I haven't seen six trees since I left home, but if I said something you folks took offense at, I take it back.'

'No, no—no offense, old buddy,' I said. I picked his hand up and shook it. 'Toni,' I said, 'Wendell here said he was sorry to think of you lying stretched out like that, and I really thought you were dead for a minute or two there, and it didn't make me feel so very good, I don't know if I ever told you.'

She reached across and ruffled my bit of hair.

As soon after supper as she could get away with it—in fact a little sooner—she stood up, looking shamefaced: she was going to leave him with us if she could.

'You going?' Wendell said. (Dumb as he was, he was the first to see it.)

'I'm sorry to run out on you-all,' she said. 'I'll see you before you leave tomorrow, Wendell. Thank you,' she said to us, 'I'll do you a favor sometime,' and she gave me and Margaret a smile, friendly but not cheerful.

'I'll give you a ride,' Wendell said.

'Thanks, my car's here.'

'No need at all for you to run off, Wendell,' I said. 'It's early. Sit right down there and I'll fix you what you've never had.'

'Murphy, it's been good talking to you,' he said. 'You

too, Mrs. Jones. Thanks for the supper.'

'Goodbye,' Margaret said.

'You're welcome, Wendell,' I said, 'but I wish you'd stay a few minutes longer.'

'Can't,' he said, 'where's my hat?'

'Nice to run into a fellow from up there,' I said. 'You take care of that good wife of yours. Tell Sterling you saw me, and if he doesn't say anything too bad about me give him my best regards. When you planning to go back?'

He winked at me. 'I'm supposed to head on back tomorrow, but with luck I might stay around a day or two and see the sights.'

Toni was behind him with her hand on the doorknob. She shook her head no and made a face.

'Well, then, with luck we'll see you again,' I said. 'But you never know about that luck stuff: sometimes a man will bow his head and pray for luck and just wind up with a stiff neck.' I rubbed my neck, since he seemed to understand sign language best. Then I shook his hand, I hope for the last time.

I saw them out, and when I went into the front room again, Margaret was sitting over by the window, half in the dark, holding a magazine. 'Better turn on the light if you want to read,' I said.

'Shh,' she said.

I walked over and looked out the window. Toni and Wendell were standing by Toni's car. Toni had her hand on the door handle, and he was standing pretty close to her. 'Shouldn't eavesdrop,' I said to Margaret.

'No,' she said. Wendell went to put his arms around Toni, and Toni backed against her car. 'Ouch,' she said.

'Those ribs,' I whispered.

'You may have to go out and pour water on him,' Margaret said.

'Goodnight,' Toni said, 'I'm going home. I'll see you tomorrow before you leave.'

'I feel like that horse that fell on you,' he said.

'You sure do,' she said. 'Look: I don't want to. Can't you understand?'

'Don't want to what?' he said.

'I don't want to do anything but go home and go to bed —all by myself.'

'Oh. Why don't you want to?'

'I just don't want to.'

'No one will ever know, Toni,' he said and pressed himself toward her.

'Will he hurt her?' Margaret said.

'No—he just hasn't got the message yet,' I said.

'My God! Not yet!?' she said.

'I don't think so.'

'It's just between me and you,' Wendell said.

'But *I* don't want to,' Toni said.

'Oh . . . you just don't want to?'

'No.'

'Oh.' He backed up a step and she started to open the car door.

'Toni,' he said, 'I just want to tell you something.'

'What?'

'I'll never forget the first time I saw you.'

'That's nice of you,' she said. 'I won't either.'

'You were with Shirley.'

'I remember.'

'And when the two of you came walking up to the barn where I was working I said to myself: "Now there's two plums," and I said to you: "Anything I can do for you girls?" and you said you were looking for a horse to buy.'

'I remember,' Toni said. 'And I asked you if you happened to know Ben Webber; you were both in the same business, and I couldn't think of anything else to say.'

'I don't remember that,' he said. 'I remember I said, "Now you girls aren't really looking for a horse, are you? I'll bet you're just out joyriding around," and you said, "A little of both." Or maybe Shirley said that. But I know for sure you were the one that couldn't stand still. You kept wiggling. I remember it because I remember saying to myself, "Now this one's more of a plum than the other one." It had to have been you because of what happened after. Because it happened with you, or I wouldn't be here now. And we had a good time, didn't we?'

'Yes,' she said.

'But now you say you don't want to, without even a reason.'

'No, I don't.'

'Maybe it's because of that judge?'

'No, I've no hard feelings.'

'That judge was enough to chill a man's ardor. I asked him, "What if I can't pay that much?" "Then bring your toothbrush next time," he said. I'll never forget it. But we had a good time right up to then. When I left I at least had a reason.' He put his hand on her shoulder and put his face up close to hers, not like he wanted to kiss her but to look in her eyes.

She didn't move a muscle, and he must have read an answer there. (I believe he was a sort of a veterinary psychologist at heart.)

'Then I won't wrestle you for it,' he said.

'No, I knew you wouldn't if you ever really understood.'

And she said goodnight, got in her car and drove away.

'What an ordeal!' Margaret said. 'I was wrong about his being sneaky.'

'Well, maybe she's got her heart set on the other one,' I said to myself. 'She talked about him enough—him and his fly eggs. Webber? Don't I know Ben Webber?'

'That Ben Webber,' I said to Margaret, 'I know him.'

'You do? What do you know about him?'

'Nothing the matter with him. Used to be a neighbor of mine. Had the eighty acres across the ditch, up home.'

'Do you remember if he came there from Los Angeles?'

'He did. In 1955. I never heard him mention any riding stables—but a person might be ashamed to have been in a business like that. He had a wife with him when he came, but she didn't last. She kept trying to get him to move back south and he wouldn't. That went on for a year and then back she went. Left him right in the middle of winter. Nice woman, too. After that he drank for maybe six months and then stopped.'

'Was he sulky?'

'Not that I ever saw. Had kind of an ingrown nature, but he was always willing to talk to a person. He didn't have red hair, either; white as Ivory Flakes, though he couldn't have been more than forty-five when I left there. Biggest part of him was his head of hair. He gave me an electric razor once—said one of his admirers gave it to him and it wouldn't cut his beard. Perfectly good razor. But I never saw him pluck off any fly eggs the way she said. Used a knife like anybody. Could be his eyesight had faded—those eggs are hard to see except in bunches; or maybe he's another Ben Webber from Los Angeles. Be a coincidence if there was two, though, let alone one. You say she has a picture?'

Margaret called Toni. I thought Toni'd be depressed: it was only twenty minutes since Wendell'd said his good-nights. But Margaret said no, if anything she was hopped up. She told Margaret Wendell made her feel like she'd won the twenty years' race in a breeze.

I couldn't make heads or tails of the conversation from Margaret's side of it, she uses so few words. 'Just a minute,' Margaret said and turned to me. 'She says Ben has a scar an inch long on the left side of his forehead, up high.'

'Could,' I said, 'I don't remember. Is she very curious?'

'He can't remember, Toni,' Margaret said. 'He wants to know if you're very curious. . . ."Not as curious as you are," she says to tell you.'

After they hung up I asked Margaret, 'Well, does she say it's the same Ben?'

'She thinks so.'

'Is she very curious?'

'Of course she is. She's going to bring his picture next time she comes over.'

First thing in the morning she brought it by.

'Couldn't wait, could you!' I said. 'Yep, that's Ben. Looks younger and better than when I knew him. Margaret tell you his wife left him for the city?'

'I don't blame her,' Toni said.

'Loved him, but she couldn't stand the weather,' I said. 'I'll bet.'

'Seemed like a good man to me. Didn't fight or drink. If I were a single woman I'd be right up there after him. Poor lonely old guy. Not a spare woman in that town, unless someone's husband has died.'

'He used to fight,' Toni said.

58

'Come to think of it, he told me so himself. Had a temper when I knew him, though I never saw him fight, or not so much a temper as a crazy streak, just a small one, didn't amount to more than five minutes a year. Even that's plenty to get yourself killed in, but he had a lot of self-restraint, too, I always thought. I wonder if he's still there. He wasn't exactly thriving on that eighty acres when I left. Didn't own it; just leased. I'll get hold of a phonebook from up there and look, unless you'd rather do it yourself?'

'That's all right,' she said. 'If you're so curious go ahead.'

WAGONTIRE

WE'D talked about it for years, and the next summer (which was last summer) we finally made a trip north to show Margaret where I was born and had lived most of my life. Margaret and I encouraged Toni to bring a man along if she wanted to. 'That'll rev old Ben's motor for him,' I told her.

And just before we left she did have one young one she said she was going to take. 'Fine,' I said, 'give him something to stand up and tell in school.' But she dropped him three days before we took off.

She didn't seem to miss him: put her feet up and took

up the whole back seat of my Chrysler by herself.

'I'll bet you're excited about seeing Ben,' I said.

'I know you like to think so,' she said.

'I remember the second or third time I talked to him,' I said. 'He'd just been moved in for a week and I said to him: "Ben, do you like to ride after cattle?"'

' "No," he said, "but I've done a lot of it. I'd be glad to help you out."

' "No, not me," I said, "I only have three and they come when I honk the horn. No, I mean for wages." And I told him I knew where there was some daywork gathering cattle up by the river—fifteen dollars a day and bring your own lunch, and that I'd be going along myself and maybe could get him the job.

' "Why, sure," he said, "I'd much appreciate that." Had nice manners I always thought, sort of a dignified old Ben. Without being stuck up. Not that he had anything to be stuck up about. Poor as a churchmouse.

'The day we went out after the cattle was the first day I saw him have a fit of temper. He came near punching a man in the jaw; and he was in no shape to be punching anyone in the jaw anymore, especially a man like the one he was about to punch, whose open hand was wide across as Ben's shoulders; why, he might have killed Ben with just a friendly slap.'

'I'll go see him if you'll promise not to talk about him all the way up,' Toni said.

'Nothing to me whether you see him or not,' I said. 'But a person has to talk about something. Anyhow that reminds me of a drowned boy I knew, not to change the subject.'

'You knew a drowned boy?'

'My best memory is of him drowned. Drowned that

64

same day. After we fished him out of the river and had him laid out to dry on the bank, Ben, Ben Webber and I, we waited there with him while Roy and Gordon went to town after a jeep. We could have packed him home easier and faster on a horse—that was how he drowned, trying to cross the river on a horse. Easy crossing, the river was low and he'd crossed it twenty times that summer in the same place and on the same horse, but this time he drowned right in the middle of it. I started to say we could have carried him out on a horse, but we thought it would be nicer for the sake of his mother not to scratch him up.

'That boy was twenty-eight years old and still lived with his mother, and he was so simple that you had to watch out for him every minute. Meant well enough, but he was always underfoot except when you wanted him for something and then you couldn't find him.

'In fact that same morning he was supposed to meet us at the café by five-thirty so we could take off to work, and it was after six when we finally found him: asleep in a stack of hay not five hundred yards from his mother's house—fast asleep on his belly with his lunch bag tucked under him in his hand, right next to his heart. I remember we had to stand him all the way up on his feet and wave some bacon under his nose to get him woke up enough to walk over on his own two feet and get up in the truck—more trouble than a horse.'

'But how did he drown?' Toni said. 'Ha—got her interested,' I said to myself.

'Well, how did he drown? We never did figure out exactly how he managed to drown. That was the question Ben got mad over, too, or a secondary question, about the cinch—whether the cinch was loose or tight. You see,

Margaret, you're ignorant of this, but a person's got to loosen the cinch before he swims his horse because a horse expands when he's swimming and the cinch will cut into him and maybe paralyze him or knock him out, which may drown him and you both.'

'Sounds like an old wives' tale to me,' Margaret said. 'Why would he expand in the water?—he should shrink.'

'Maybe you're right,' I said. 'I was never foolish enough to try to verify it. So just before we crossed the river, when the cattle were already in the water, the three of us—this boy Larry and Ben and me—got off to loosen our cinches. Roy and Gordon had already crossed and were up on the far bank looking at us. We all kept an eye on Larry. Ben had only seen him for the first time that morning, but even he'd already noticed that he needed watching over. Ben was the closest to him, but every one of us saw him get off. Myself, I just took it for granted that, even foolish as the boy was, if he remembered to get off he couldn't help but remember to loosen the cinch— since why else would he get off? Anyhow, we even saw him fiddle with the cinch, and as I say, Ben was the closest one to him.

'Then we rode into the water. You know I can't swim, so I was looking at my horse's ears and thinking about my own affairs, when I heard Ben yell. (Never a peep out of Larry.)

'I looked around and saw no Larry and no horse, then the horse's legs came up out of the water and he rolled over two or three turns like a barrel, washed over into shallow water, and when his feet struck bottom he floundered and staggered and got up on them and clambered up the far bank—just the horse. By then Roy had his boots off and was in the water. He could swim and so could Ben. Gordon and I got in too, and wallowed around to the best of our ability. But he was always an awful hard boy to find when you wanted him, and when Roy pulled him out he was white as a rabbit and wasn't breathing. We pumped a few cupfuls of water out of him, but that was all—couldn't get him to draw a breath.

'It wasn't what we'd had in mind, and no one knew what to say except curse a little. Half our clothes were wet, and there wasn't a dry sock among us, so Ben pulled his boots on over his bare feet and went off gathering sticks for a fire. It was a nice sunny fall day as I remember —little chilly.

'The cattle drifted off and we just watched them go— had to come back and start all over the next day.

'I remember the horse Larry'd been riding had rubbed up against one of the others and was standing with his back hunched, shivering, and kept shaking his head and neck to try to get the water out of his ears. He was all right but he looked like he felt pretty miserable. Roy said we ought to pull the saddle off of him, and he tiptoed over on his bare feet and uncinched him and pulled it off. And right at that moment no one thought to wonder whether the cinch was loose or tight, or anyone who did never said.

'Roy dragged the saddle over by where Gordon was building the fire; we propped up some sticks to hang our clothes on so they'd dry faster, and we tore apart some sage, made a bed near the fire and carried Larry to it, so he'd dry out top and bottom. We could have undressed him and dried his clothes faster, but we talked ourselves out of it.

'With things organized like that, we were pretty well over the shock of it, and Roy said we might as well eat, long as we had to wait to dry out anyway. Ben fished out his watch and said, "Yep, it's past noon." So we untied our sack lunches from our saddles. I noticed Ben just nibbled at his. I thought then it was the drowning, but he was always like that. I spent three years watching him suffer over that stomach of his; he took pills, and you'd think taking a pill was the most shameful thing in the world to watch him—and nothing in them but baking soda; but I started to say I knew him three years before he admitted out loud that he had anything the matter with him. A nervous stomach he called it, whatever that is.

'Anyhow, he nibbled his and I bit right into mine, which naturally led me to think of Larry, since he loved his lunch so. "Last thing I heard him say was 'How close is it to noon?' " I said and nodded toward the body.

' "That's the last thing he said to me, too," Ben said.

' "Usually said it three or four times," Roy said. "Sure liked his lunch."

' "He'd mash it though," Gordon said.

' "Wasn't because he didn't like it," Roy said, "just the opposite."

' "I know it," Gordon said.

' "I noticed this morning, he was camped right on top of his lunchbag," Ben said.

' "That's what he liked best of all," I said, "his lunch and lunchtime. We used to say to him: 'Larry, when are you going to stop asking when's lunch?' 'After lunch,' he'd say, and laugh."

' "I didn't think he had that much wit," Ben said.

' "Roy here taught him the answer. Might as well untie the lunch from his saddle. Make his mother feel bad to send it back."

' "Sure, Murphy—must be soaked through anyway," Roy said.

' "Damn, look at the way he tied it on," I said, "all but cut it in two with the saddle strings. Wanted to make sure he never lost it."

' "He always tied it down like that," Roy said. "I said to him one morning when we were starting out, 'Larry, would you like me to show you a way to tie your lunch to your saddle without mashing it?' 'Sure!' he said, 'Thanks, Roy.' So I tied it on for him. But the lesson didn't take."

' "He had a passion for cinching things down," Gordon said.

' "How do you mean?" Ben said. I suppose there was something in his tone but none of us noticed it.

' "Did he loosen his cinch before he went in the water?" Gordon said.

' "I was watching him," Ben said, almost mumbled it.

' "I know he got off and fooled with it," Gordon said.

' "What else would the poor boy be doing, Gordon," I said, "if he wasn't loosening it?"

' "Pulling it tight," Gordon said.

' "Without thinking, you mean?"

' "Without or with, either way—wasn't much of a thinker."

' "Seems unlikely," I said.

' "Seems unlikely the horse would roll over in the water and drown him," Gordon said.

' "That's true, too," I said. We were busy philosophizing and looking at the body and didn't look at Ben at all. "Well, what's the verdict, Roy?" I said. "You pulled the saddle off. Did you happen to notice?" But when I looked up at Roy he gave his head a little shake like a man with a fly on his nose, which seemed to mean we should shut our mouths. Gordon and I turned and looked at Ben—looked strange, had his head down, hiding his face behind his hat. All of a sudden he jumped up on his feet. "I told you I was keeping an eye on him!"—red in the face and opening and closing both his hands like a machine—but he kept them down by his sides. Roy and I just opened our mouths and looked at him. But Gordon stood up and started waving his arm. "Oh, wait now," Gordon said, "I couldn't see from where I was, and I never meant to think you weren't keeping an eye on him. If you saw him loosen his cinch, he loosened his cinch. I'd never have doubted it if I understood that's what you meant to say."

' "Horse may have stepped on a rock under the water and the rock turned, lost his footing," I said.

' "Sure may have," Gordon said.

' "I believe that cinch *was* loose now that I think about it," Roy said.

'Ben had his mouth open like he wanted to say something. Then his hands started to slow down; we couldn't keep from staring at them; he looked at us and then down at himself and made one stop (the one he looked at; the other one went on for a few more strokes; then he stopped it too and gave his head a shake). "Sorry," he said. "Misunderstanding."

' "All a misunderstanding, friend," Gordon said. "Think nothing of it and I won't either," and he tiptoed over to Ben on his bare feet and put his big hand out for Ben to shake, which Ben did. Poor Ben turned white in the face then, sat back down and shook his head, and a minute later he said, "I feel about half sick."

'Later on, when he and I were there alone, he told me

he figured he was a little touched. A man would challenge him, or do something he took that way, and he'd go almost blind mad for a minute or two. But he said he hadn't actually hit anyone for years. Good thing, because a man wants to be careful who he hits.

'Now that I think about it, he told me that the last fight he'd been in and the one he thought cured him took place there in Los Angeles. But that time unless he was lying the fellow really did challenge him. Slapped Ben's girlfriend's face for no reason at all—except to try to make Ben fight. Friendly gesture like that would be hard to misinterpret, wouldn't you say? And from what Ben said, it worked well for the man, if that was what he wanted.'

'He wasn't lying, Murphy,' Toni said, about half amused.

'No? Some bird gave you a slap for no reason?—and Ben coldcocked him?'

'That's right.'

'Well, if Margaret and I had been there with you we'd have done the same thing Ben did. I'll tell you, you Los Angeles people are too western for me. I'll never move that far south. Why in the world did the man want to slap you? The one Ben gave him back almost killed him— unless Ben told me a story.'

'It almost did. He hit his head on a table edge, and they wouldn't let Ben out of jail until he woke up. He was unconscious for three days, and Ben said afterward that he promised himself while he was sitting in there that if he ever got out he wouldn't fight again for anything—not even for a beautiful woman like me. I don't know why he slapped me. He was Ben's landlord—he owned the riding stables. He'd given Ben a lease, and for some reason he wanted to kick him out before the lease was up, and Ben wouldn't leave. Anyway, they didn't like each other. He came up to us in a bar that was only a few hundred yards from the stables—he owned the bar, too—and told Ben to take off his hat. There were six or seven men lined up at the bar all with their hats on, like always, so Ben just shrugged and turned away and tried to start talking to someone else—and he slapped me.'

'Did it break the lease?'

'Yes, Ben was afraid to stay there after that; he thought the man might try to have him killed or who knows what. So he moved to another stables. It's too bad: he never made as much money anywhere as he did at that place.'

'Well, a person has to admire him for his self-restraint, generally speaking,' I said.

'I don't,' she said. 'What about people who don't have temper tantrums in the first place?'

'Nothing admirable about that,' I said.

'I still like it better.'

'You like it better, but here you are still nursing a grudge for Ben; and how long's it been—twenty years? So how do you explain that? Bad luck?'

'Maybe he deserves it,' she said.

'Maybe he does,' I said, 'but there's more to that grudge than just a grudge, if you take my meaning.'

'I don't, but don't explain it,' she said.

'You don't, like heck,' I thought, 'but maybe I'd better shut my mouth—seems to be rubbing her the wrong way.' 'Margaret, you haven't said a word.'

'No, I've been listening, though. What are those wooden fences for, that don't go anywhere? Look.'

'Drift fences—to keep the snow from blowing over onto the road. You've seen them before, surely.'

72

'But it's so barren here. Does it really snow that much?'
'It does. It really snows,' I said.

* * *

We stayed overnight in Reno and went on north in the morning. I told them we'd be there before noon. Margaret looked out at the landscape and kept looking at it and began to get a little nervous. 'Is it this flat and empty around where we're going? It's not, is it?'

'Oh, no, we're only forty-five hundred feet here. Up there it's sixty-five hundred and a regular park. Make Pearblossom look like the Sahara. It's desert—I would have moved out right after I was born if it wasn't—but it's a lush desert, not like here, though it's sort of like here. Lots of irrigation water, though, comes down from the mountains. Flat cultivated ground around town and, beyond that, desert and more desert, then a mountain or two, and more desert. Red rocks, juniper trees, sagebrush, black rocks, bunch grass, an awful lot of lava rock, some of it just like broken glass; you'll be crazy about it. Winter lasts from November through June and there's no spring at all, except some people like to call the first day of summer spring, when the grass jumps up about six inches. But if we're not unlucky we'll catch summer there. Generally we don't have a hard frost till August, though to tell the truth I've seen it drop to ten degrees on the Fourth of July; people argue over whether that's a late frost or an early one. See off that way?'

'What? I don't see anything.'

'That's where Wendell lives. If we had a helicopter we could drop in. Say, shall we get a room or stay with

73

someone? I know half a dozen people who wouldn't dare squawk.'

'I'd just as soon get a room,' Toni said.

'So would I,' Margaret said.

'I would, too,' I said.

There was a new motel, built since I'd left, on the north end of town (we could see it from the south end); we rented rooms, then walked back downtown to eat. Couldn't go fifteen feet without meeting someone: 'Is that Murphy Jones? I thought that was you.' 'Yep, and I'd like for you to meet my wife, Margaret, and this is Margaret's niece, Toni Wilson.' Half the time I couldn't remember their names, people I'd known for fifty years; should have paged through a phone book ahead of time.

When we came back out of the café I stopped on the sidewalk. 'Want a rubberneck tour now that you're acclimated?' I said. 'Or shall we run right out and see Ben?'

'A tour,' Toni said.

'Okay. This street is the main street. The other café is over there—you see the sign? And down where the flag is there, is the post office; and there where it says Dry Goods, that's my old store; and over there where it says Groceries, that's an exaggeration; and there's the hotel: if we'd had to we could have stayed there. Want to go see Ben now?'

'What a tour!' Toni said.

'Well, I'm anxious to see if he's married again.'

'Is this a good time?' she asked. 'Maybe we should call first? That's the easiest way to find out if he's married anyway, if that's all you want to know; or ask someone.'

'Let's just drive over,' I said. 'Best time of day to find him in the house, just before one.'

'We'll get no peace until we do, Toni,' Margaret said.

'I don't mind,' Toni said. 'Let's get it over with. I'm kind of curious myself.'

'Unless you'd rather take the car and go over on your own?' I said.

'No thanks.'

It was just a couple of miles. We turned off the county road—good graveled road that ran along below the raised bank of the irrigation canal—into his lane, which was all potholes. There was pasture on both sides of the lane, and down about a quarter mile we could see his house and yard, with the old garden orchard in front of it. There was pasture grass under the trees, and when we got closer we saw a couple of baby veal calves out eating. Off a ways we could see the barn and a couple of sheds and twenty or thirty cattle out in the fields, and the remains of a haypile. Just an ordinary small stock farm with a small square house on it: nothing fancily kept up or very rundown either.

As we pulled into the yard a blue-and-gray bobtailed shepherd dog squeezed himself out from under the porch and started barking.

'Maybe he won't be home,' Toni said.

'He is. Car's here and so's his truck,' I said.

'Is that the same car he had when you knew him? It looks like it should be,' Margaret said.

'Same one. Same truck, too. You don't see many like that anymore. Hasn't got rich, evidently. Different dog, though.'

I opened the car door a crack and he came loping at us with his dander up, yapping and growling. 'If he was out in the fields the dog'd be with him,' I said.

'He won't bite, will he?' Margaret said.

'I don't know why not. Let's wait a minute and see if Ben comes out.'

We waited.

'He must not be home,' Toni said. 'Too bad, Murphy! I wish I had an apple.'

'Almost got to be,' I said. 'Probably doesn't sleep good by himself at night and conks out at noon.'

'That dog would have waked up anyone by now,' Margaret said.

'Should have. I hesitated to say so because I don't want to hurt Toni in the romantic part of her feelings, but when I left here Ben was a little deaf in one ear.'

'Well, he has two, I hope,' Margaret said.

'He has, but if he fell asleep sitting up on a chair with his head flopped over against his shoulder, he might be deaf to the world—I hesitate to say so.'

'That's all right,' Toni said, 'but I don't think he's home.'

'Let's sit here one more minute, then if no one comes out one of us can go knock on the door.'

'I'll do it right now. I want an apple anyway.' And before I could restrain her she stepped out of the car. The dog advanced a little, up on his toes and puffed up like a lion. She picked a rock up. 'Blue, go lie down,' she said.

I thought I'd get to see him hit with a rock, but he turned and trotted off; still growling and with his back up, but he was headed in the other direction—did my heart good to see it. Then he started twisting his head back over his shoulder first on one side and then the other, grinning at her with his ears pressed back flat, like he wanted her to either hit him or love him. Seemed to be possessed of seven feelings at once, fearful obedience being the one I liked best. 'It's always handy to travel with an animal trainer,' I said to Margaret. We waited to get out until he squeezed himself all the way back up in under the porch where he came from.

Toni knocked on the door, waited, and then pounded on it. By the time Margaret and I got there she had her nose against the front-room window.

'People get shot doing that,' I told her.

'His living room looks like a tackroom,' she said.

'That's a relief,' I said. 'Here I was scared to death he might have found another woman.'

'Let's see,' Margaret said. 'My, yes! He hasn't held many tea parties.'

'Let's see,' I said. 'Why's he keep his bridles in the house, I wonder?'

'So the mice won't chew them,' Toni said. 'He had it happen once. The mice in a house don't get as hungry.'

'One mouse thirty years ago and he carries his bridles to the house ever after,' I said. 'I'll bet he's got more twists in him that won't come out than a grapevine. Awful fine man, though. The house isn't very dirty, I wouldn't say, would you? Just cluttered.'

'Look at all those magazines on the table,' Margaret said.

'Probably been piling them up there for a year,' I said, 'along with his bills. Neat stacks, though.'

'I don't see where he finds room to sit down and eat,' Margaret said.

'There in the armchair,' Toni said. 'Look, there's a plate on it.'

'Not much of an eater anyway,' I said. 'I wonder where he is; couldn't be far. He may show up any minute.'

Toni looked behind her. 'Let's go,' she said.

'We can come back later,' I said. 'We found out the

main thing; it's all plain sailing now.' She didn't seem to hear me.

'Murphy, I just thought of something,' she said, and she pointed. 'That's your house on the other side of the canal —you said you lived across the ditch and that's the only other house around here. But you haven't said a thing about it.'

'That's it.'

'Aren't you going to show it to us?' Margaret said. 'You lived there for sixty years.'

'Off and on,' I said. So I had to promise to call the man who lived there and arrange to show it to them. She climbed over the fence and picked some apples. Then I took them for a drive out in the country. Showed them a creek and a lake, some hieroglyphs, antelope—gave them a regular tour. We must have gone a hundred miles. On the way out we didn't see a soul, just a few tire tracks. But on the way back we passed a man on horseback driving a range cow in front of him. 'He must be taking her over to the corrals at Dry Lake,' I said, 'just a couple of miles from here.'

When we got closer, 'Say, that's Roy Hill,' I said. 'You mind waiting for him at the corrals? Might as well say hello. Toni can question him about Ben.'

'I will,' she said, and laughed.

'If she's dissimulating she's doing it better than she usually does,' I thought. 'Sure doesn't seem very excited. If she'd pretend not to even be curious, that would be a sign, but she doesn't, just acts natural. I can't make it out.'

They didn't mind, so we got out of the car at the corrals and sat down on the fence in the sun. It was a nice day, getting on in the afternoon but still warm enough to sit out without a coat.

'Roy Hill—that's a familiar name,' Margaret said.

'I mentioned him to you: he's the one who fished Larry out of the water—the foreman. I'll tell you another little thing I remember. We were waiting for Larry at the café that morning—he'd already made us a half hour late, and just when we were about to call his mother someone came in and told us he was asleep in the haystack a few hundred yards from home. "Well, that's typical," Roy said. "We'll just stop by and load him up and go on from there. He'll miss his breakfast and serve him right for making us late—damn him anyway. . . . Well, maybe I'll get a couple of doughnuts just to stuff in his mouth and keep him quiet." So he stood up to go over to the counter and order the doughnuts, and in the five seconds it took him to get there he'd changed his mind again and he ordered him a whole breakfast—ham and hotcakes and eggs with the yolks fried hard, which was the only way Larry would eat them. I'll always remember that.'

'He sounds like a nice man,' Toni said.

'As good a hearted man as ever lived. Single last time I saw him, but I'm afraid he'll stay that way: In love with his brother's wife for years. Twenty years while she was alive and since she died he's true to her memory—though the brother himself remarried.'

'Doesn't sound like my type,' Toni said.

'No, lives like a monk. Here he comes now.'

Roy was about fifty-five—short and slight and sort of daintily made, but wore like rubber. Looked almost like he had eight years ago.

He corraled his cow and got off his horse, and I made the introductions. After some small talk about the cow (seemed she'd bore dead calves three years in a row, so he was getting her in to sell), I said to him: 'Roy, Margaret here asked who you were a while ago—and we got to talking and I happened to mention the way you ordered breakfast for that boy Larry the same day he drowned. He was asleep in that little stack of hay there on the town end of his mother's lane and we took it to him there. Do you remember that?'

'Let's see now . . . we found him asleep in that hay all right. Poor kid; how'd you happen to be thinking of that, though, after all this time?'

'Well, we were just talking as people will, and got to talking about the time when—'

'Do you remember when Ben Webber lost his temper that day?' Margaret said. No patience at all.

'Quite a Ben, I'll say,' Roy said. 'Darned if he's not. Sure do. I remember that. Took it into his head to challenge another fellow there—Gordon. Coming on top of that drowning like it did it always stuck in my mind.'

'Toni here's a friend of Ben's,' I said.

'The heck she is!' and he turned to her and touched the front of his hat.

'Uh huh,' Toni said.

'Quite a Ben, I'll say,' Roy said.

'She knew him years ago in Los Angeles,' I said. 'To tell the truth she rode all the way up here in the car with Margaret and me just to go and take a look at him.'

'Oh, Murphy.'

'Have you been in to see him today, then?' Roy said.

'Uh—we stopped out at his place,' I said, 'but there—'

'In where?' Toni said.

'Uh, he had to be operated on,' Roy said. 'He had an operation. I thought maybe you'd come up because of it, from what Murphy said. But he's all right.'

'What was wrong with him?' Toni said, calm as calm. I was watching her like a hawk.

'Hemorrhaged ulcers. He had indigestion—had it for years. The doctor said his stomach was in an awful mess. But he came along fine once they'd operated. For a couple of weeks after, they made him swill a lot of gruel—but you know even that was more than he could do before. No one knew it, but he had himself so weak from not eating or not keeping down what he ate that we finally almost lost him. But now he can eat whatever he wants, and says he feels better these last two weeks than any time in the last ten or twelve years.'

'How long has he been in the hospital?' Margaret said.

'Three and a half weeks, and due to come home day after tomorrow. The doctor told me that operation may have made a new man of him, take a while to tell. But to hear Ben talk it already has.'

'The doctor said that?' I said.

'The doctor's really that optimistic?' Margaret said.

'I'm glad to be the one to say so,' Roy said. 'Hard little nut, too, that doctor. He called Ben a fool to his face for not having it taken care of years ago. Ben told him he'd never been to a doctor all that time. But Ben told me he did go to one once ten years ago—and they told him then he needed an operation. So he never would go back. I didn't tell the doctor that. Don't tell Ben I told you some of this.'

'We won't. How'd the old burro finally end up in the hospital at all? I don't imagine he had sense enough to take himself there.'

'Time he had the sense he didn't have the strength. I went by to pick him up one morning to go do some cow work. Found his horse all saddled and ready to go, tied to a post out in front of the house. He'd got out and got his chores done and got back to the house and was lying on his back on the couch. Mumble and groan was about all he could do. He was hurting, I'll tell you—sweat rolling off of him; had blood all over his chin; I didn't see it at first, reddish-colored as he is and with about a three-day stubble. Surprised me when I saw it. He asked me to get him a glass of water and call the doctor, and when I said I thought I should take him in to the hospital he didn't say no— I'll say not—wanted something for that pain. Had a belly on him like a plank.'

'What was the operation?' Toni said.

'Cut out the bad part of his stomach and left the good, about all I understand of it. But the doctor told me afterward anyone who'd ever butchered a sheep could have done it. He didn't do it himself, though. "I'll have my fishing partner operate," he told me.

'They were afraid he'd die if they didn't hurry and go into him, or die from the shock if they did, as little strength as he had. So they tried to build him up for three or four days, and I guess they did, some, but the doctor told me it was like trying to fill up a sieve.

'Wasn't much to him: when I walked him out to the car to take him in that morning, he didn't feel like he weighed a hundred pounds, and you know he's six feet tall.'

'It's very nice for Ben that you're around,' Margaret said.

'Handy, but he'd have got over to the phone and called someone if he needed to—didn't have to since he knew I was coming.'

'I don't think that's what Margaret meant,' Toni said.

82

'Ben's lucky to have someone around who's willing to take such an interest.'

'Why, sure,' Roy said. 'Gets dull in there without company, especially if you're halfway well like he is now. He'll be glad to see you folks. If you go in tonight, if it's not inconvenient maybe I can send something by you.'

'Fine,' I said. 'What you want us to take?'

'Food. I got quite a kick out of him. I called him on the phone one night a week ago and said I was coming into town and did he want me to bring anything, his mail or something to read? But that was the day the doctor had told him he could eat whatever he wanted from now on. And he said if I could would I stop by a hamburger stand and if there wasn't too long a line to bring him a double order of french fries and some ketchup?—just like a twelve-year-old boy. I had a little trouble getting by the nurse with it; but it didn't seem to hurt him, so now there's two or three of us send in something when we get the chance.'

Then Toni mumbled something about not knowing whether she wanted to go in to the hospital to visit him —maybe she'd wait till he was home. Too deep for me.

We talked till it started to get cold, then we decided to follow Roy back to Ben's place and help him do the chores. When we were all four standing by my car, after he'd loaded his horse and cow and we were all about to take off, he raised his arm and pointed across the flat. We were facing north and could see Bly Mountain off sixty or seventy miles, sticking up, and Horse Mountain, which isn't much of a mountain, about ten miles, and a lot of sagebrush and juniper flat (looked like a lot, but they say a man on foot if he's six feet tall and looking out across flat ground can see less than three miles of the round world—after that it's all sky). 'Well, what's the old country look like to you, Murphy? You picked the best time of year to come, I'll say.'

'Only time,' I said.

'Only time. I'll say,' he said. 'We had a fifteen-degree frost the last day of June—bet it doesn't surprise you. Murphy's the only grown person from here who ever took it into his head to leave. But darned if I don't think now you did the right thing, Murphy, after all.' And he touched his hat and looked at Margaret. Took her by surprise and for a couple of seconds she didn't understand him. Then she chuckled out loud, which she does about once a year.

'Thank you,' she said.

'The old devil only talks to three women a year out here, but he knows what to say when he sees one,' I thought to myself.

Toni spent the whole twenty miles back to Ben's annoying me. At first I was glad to see she was nervous, but by the time five minutes went by I decided it wasn't worth it. I hate it when they can't make up their minds. 'Take your time,' I told her, 'you don't have to decide right now. We have a couple of hours yet.'

'I don't think it would be right to inflict myself on him while he's trapped there in the hospital.'

'Nobody's said you had to,' I said to myself, 'and if he can't stand it he can do what you did to Lyle and just roll over. But make up your mind.' 'When you make your mind up just let me know,' I said, 'Doesn't matter to me what we do, just so we do something.'

But they wouldn't let me alone. Margaret wasn't much better. 'Maybe Murphy should call Ben,' she said. 'All right, I'm willing,' I said. Toni liked that idea, so then they began to worry about what I should say. They decided I should say we were in town and to mention Toni as being along—and see what his tone was. If he didn't sound unfriendly toward her, then I should go on and try to sound him out further.

I said all right, and then they started giving me instructions about what I should or shouldn't say depending on what he did or didn't say and how he said it.

If when I said Toni was along he said, 'Oh, she is!' like his heart was full of joy, that was one thing, and if he said, 'Oh . . . she *is?*' in a civil way, that was another, and if he said it as if he'd just been told it hailed on the barley, that was a third. 'Damn, they must think I'm dumb,' I thought. 'But what if I sneeze and he says "Whiskey!" what'll I do then?' I said.

'What do you mean?' Toni said.

'No, you know, just in case?' Then she started in to apologize, and I had to listen to that for a while.

'No, no, that's all right,' I said, 'but if you don't mind I'm going to call him as soon as we get to his place so I don't have to listen to you women all evening.'

'Okay, but I don't want to be in the room when you call,' Toni said.

'Fine, I'll suffer it,' I said.

Roy let me into Ben's house, and I called and talked to him while they went out to start the chores. Then I walked out to the barn.

Roy had one of Ben's cows in the stanchion and the two calves we'd seen out in the orchard were nursing her, one on each side. A cat, a half-wild-looking affair, was squatted down seven or eight feet away from the cow and as far away from the people as she could get, meowing. Seems Ben had the habit of squirting milk to her.

The two women were sitting beside each other on a bale of hay, and Roy was occupying himself raking some litter out of the way while he waited for the calves to have their suck.

'I got hold of him,' I said.

'What did he say?' Toni said.

'What are you so excited about? First of all he said hello —not in too friendly a tone of voice, either, to tell the truth. Then I said, "Hello, Ben? This is Murphy Jones." "By golly it is," he said, "how are you Murphy?" "Can't complain," I said, "just up in the old country on a vacation and said to myself, 'I'll stop in to see Ben,' so we did, my wife and I and a friend of ours—my wife's niece; we stopped by your place—didn't see anyone around but the dog and he wasn't too friendly. So then we ran into old Roy later, and he—"'

'Come on, Murphy—what did he say when you mentioned my name?—or did you ever mention it?'

'Murphy,' Roy said, 'I've got some water to look at outside. Soon as these calves have her sucked dry and start batting her with their heads could you shove them into this pen here for me?—he keeps them here at night —and turn the cow out of the barn?'

'Sure will,' I said. 'Now there's a discreet man,' I said after he went out. 'Didn't want to witness your privacies. We're pretty near all like that up here.'

'Damn you,' she said. Worth the trouble it took to excite her just to get to see her eyes light up and her face get pink and hear her raise her voice.

'What'd he say when I mentioned your name? He said, "Who's that? Can't place her." No, he didn't really. He knew you right off. When he heard your name he snarled like a big brown bear.'

'I wouldn't doubt it,' she said.

'Then there was a terrible noise. I didn't know what it was at first, but he had bit the mouthpiece off from the receiver, now that he can eat whatever he wants.'

'Come on, what did he say?' Margaret said.

'When I mentioned her name? Why, the man was delighted, far as I could tell, which was pretty well.'

'Just tell us what he said,' Margaret said.

' "She *is!* The hell you say!" that's what he said—almost hit high C.'

They both looked me in the eye to see if I was lying, and I wasn't too sure myself by the time they got done.

' "Yep, she's here. I'm married to her aunt," I told him. Then I told him we'd like to see him, either in there or at home, whichever he'd like better. I told him Roy said he'd be home in a day or two.'

' "I sure hope to be, but there's no reason to wait till then," he said. "If you're not afraid of hospitals come on in first chance you get; come up tonight. You'd better warn her I'm in awful shape to be looked at by a woman who hasn't seen me in twenty years." '

'I'm sure that's the truth,' Toni said.

' "But I won't look any better at home," he said. So I said to him:

' "Well, I don't think it's for that reason, but she is a little apprehensive about coming in. She wants to see you, sure does, but she wanted me to ask you if in all honesty you might not like it better if she waited till you were home again."

' "If she'd prefer that, that's all right," he said, "but you tell her I'd be tickled pink to have her come in. Might even find something to comb my hair with."

' "I'm sure she'll want to then, Ben," I told him.'

'Murphy—he wouldn't say "tickled pink." '

'He did, I'll swear by it. You may not like it but that's what the old feller said. Could be he has you mixed up with somebody else.'

'Maybe he does. Did you tell him my last name?'

'Yes, I told him your last name and he told it to me back. Now aren't you something!'

Roy came back into the barn and she dropped the subject. But soon as we were back in the car (we were going to meet Roy at the café and eat with him and then go on to the hospital, which was in the bigger town about fifteen miles from ours) she asked me: 'Did Ben say anything else?'

'Just to slow down at the first hamburger stand on the right coming into Klamath Falls, and if the line isn't too long to stop and get him their biggest hamburger.'

'He thinks there'll be lines at all the hamburger stands,' Margaret said.

'He made me promise to let him pay for it. I told him we were going out to eat and it wouldn't be any trouble to bring him in a decent meal if he'd like one; and he said that was the decentest meal there was, and he'd been thinking about one all day even while he was eating. I asked him was the hospital food pretty bad? "No, not half bad," he said.'

'Talk about inalienable rights,' Margaret said. 'To be hungry year in and year out and not to be able to eat what you want and what other people eat, or to suffer afterward every time you try to—what a trial that must be.'

'Make a person feel sorry for himself all right,' I said. 'Not much glory in an ulcer, either. People even blame you for getting it.'

'I blame him,' Toni said. 'I wonder if he'll develop another one?'

'Could,' I said. 'Right now I'd say he's like a person who just pulled a wrinkle out of his sock: feels good not to feel bad. But before long maybe he'll go to fretting again and start a brand-new ulcer. Or he may be serene as I am from this time on. How old exactly is he?'

'Fifty-three,' Toni said.

'Fifty-three? That's early. But then there's been a lot of wear and tear; serenity may set in a little early with him. Hard to say, hard to say. You'd better ask the doctor, or better yet just marry him and see—doesn't cost much. Then if he gets sick again or starts acting up, you drop him like a hot potato—that's my recommendation.'

'Did I ask you a question, Murphy? I didn't mean to.'

'Or you could propose one of those trial marriages that you like.'

'Do I have to decide now or can I wait until after I see him?'

'Doesn't make a bit of difference,' I said, 'but on second thought I doubt if he'd go for a trial marriage.'

We left her off at the hospital at eight-thirty. She asked us to come in with her, but Margaret said no. Visiting hours lasted till ten, and I told her we'd be back then. 'Oh, sooner than that,' she said.

'No, no sooner,' I said. 'It'll pass. Just hand him that hamburger and everything will be all right.'

'Well, I can always say I have to leave and come down to the lobby,' she said.

Margaret and I went downtown to a place I knew and watched some people dance. You couldn't hear yourself think, but I said to her: 'I can't make her out.'

'She doesn't want you to.'

'I know that. But she just doesn't seem excited enough. She should be all wrought up.'

'Why should she be?'

'She's trailed him right to the side of his bed,' I said.

'Well, maybe she is mostly just curious, right now,' Margaret said.

'Well, she ought to be wrought up, in my opinion.'

Margaret smiled.

'What's so funny about that?' I said.

'You think it's Toni that's wrong, and not your opinion —that's funny,' she said.

We walked into the lobby at ten. After a couple of minutes she came down, looking just like she had when she went up.

'How'd it go?' I said.

'Okay—we had a nice visit.'

'Find him a new man?'

'New to me. He says you should come up. They're not very strict about the hours.'

'We'll have to to find out anything. Want to, Margaret?'

'Okay. Do you think we should, Toni? You haven't worn him out?'

'No, he seems fine. I'll come with you.'

If he'd run a comb through his hair I couldn't tell it. He'd shaved though. His tan was gone and it left him pink as a rose.

Given that high-colored complexion and blue eyes and the white hair, he was a colorful-looking individual; one of a kind, for whatever that's worth. I may have been prejudiced, but when I shook his hand I couldn't help thinking that if *I* was a good-looking woman with the power of choice I might wonder what I was doing here, now that I'd come so far. Even without prejudice, his arm was so thin you could see the parts move, and I thought at the time that if I was him I'd have kept it covered up: He always had when I knew him.

We said how good it was to see each other, and I introduced him to Margaret. 'Mrs. Jones,' he said to her (and stuck out his hand, arm and all), 'I hope you don't mind being on the receiving end of a little gratitude: you seem to be the cause of this reunion.' (Like I said to Margaret later, if he'd gone past the eighth grade we'd have needed a translator; sounded like a rehearsed speech, but Margaret seemed to like it all right.)

'I am?' she said. 'Well, in a roundabout way I guess I am!'

'The last person I dreamed I'd see come through that door was Toni,' he said. 'Even after Murphy called I found it hard to believe till it happened. Have you been enjoying your vacation so far?'

'Yes, thanks, so far it's been interesting. Toni and Murphy have talked so much about you on the way up I feel as if I already know you. You're not quite as I pictured you, but almost.'

'I'll bet she told you I growled at her the last time I saw her. That's what she told me she remembers best, but I only remembered it after she reminded me.'

'You probably remember the time she growled at you,' Margaret said, 'if she ever did.'

'Oh, she did, she did,' he said, and he winked. 'I remember every time I was mistreated back to the year one.'

All three of them beaming like they ran on batteries. 'Winking as does it,' I thought. 'If I wasn't an honest man I'd try it myself. I wonder if they like him for himself alone or because of what he says? Either one's hard to believe, from an objective point of view.' 'That's how it is, Ben, all right,' I said.

'I hadn't lost track of her,' Ben said. 'I'm always looking for her ads in the magazines. Is she much of a horse trainer, Murphy? I asked her but I couldn't get her to say. I know in the old days we had trouble finding a horse quick enough to keep underneath her.' He winked at me.

'Has the opposite fault now, Ben,' I said. 'Won't fall even when the time's ripe. Can't pry her loose.'

'She told me one all but flattened her last summer.'

'I think they're trying to tease me,' Toni said.

'That's a fine picture you advertise with sometimes—do you know the one I mean? That mare is up on her toes like this.' (He cocked his arms on the sheet.) 'Is she one you trained yourself?'

She nodded like a girl picked out for praise in school, and he kept on looking at her with a grin on his face till she lowered her eyes.

He had the bed jacked up, so he was sitting almost straight up and resting back against three pillows, the upper two behind his head (must have been in good with the nurses to get so many). His pocket watch was hanging by a string from the top rung of the bedstead. He rolled his head and glanced at the watch without raising himself or even lifting his head from the pillow. I'll bet he made that same gesture a hundred times a day lying in there. Seen from the side his face was all corners: sharp cheekbones and a straight sharp nose and a chin like the end of a brick—four-cornered chin—rawboned fellow for sure, even if he'd been fat.

'He'll come with quite a dowry of bills,' I thought, 'after four weeks in the hospital.' I tried to think of something friendly to say but nothing came to me right off. Then while I was looking at his face I had an unbefitting impulse, and it dawned on me: 'You're having a freak of jealousy, that's what's the matter with you; still don't see what they see in him, though.'

'Nurse is going to come in and chase you all out in a minute,' he said. 'Hope you're going to be around the country for a while, Murphy.'

'No very definite plans,' I said. 'Margaret won't let me make any and Toni agrees to everything in the world except what she doesn't want to . . . and that's very little —I just mean to say you're good-natured.' Didn't come out right, but anyhow the nurse had appeared in the doorway and they were all looking at her.

'One minute,' Ben said and held up a finger.

'I'll give you two but that's all,' she said.

'Looks like you have pretty good jailers here,' I said in a friendly way; proud of myself, but he didn't seem to hear me.

'Let me tell you something foolish,' he said, and turned his head to look at his watch. 'In the afternoons I'll lie here and do some wishful thinking. I hate to say how small my thoughts get—just who might come in and what they might bring—magazines to look at, hardly ever think past evening; mostly of what they might bring to eat, to be honest,' and he laughed and turned redder in the face and waved that arm. (I told Margaret later I'd never heard the man chatter so. Thought he had to say it all at once.) 'And then I'll play "will I, won't I" as to whether I'll get what I want or not.'

'I don't blame you,' I said.

'But today I worked myself into a bind. There were two people I could think of who might come in. Everyone's farming night and day this month and I'm about to get out of this place anyway, so company's slacked off. The upshot is, one of these two called and indicated he wasn't coming in and also happened to mention that the other party had gone down to Likely after a bull. So neither one was coming and they were the complete list. Now if I'd known to start with they weren't coming I'd have made different calculations, just to leave myself something to amuse myself hoping for. But the list was law once I'd made it. So there wasn't a chance in the world anything could happen today—had to wait till tomorrow; which was a strange feeling, not sure I ever had it before. Because as I say I'll generally allow myself something to wish for anyhow. Of course a sensible person could just say to himself, "That's foolish, anything can happen." But you lie around alone and talk to yourself long enough and you begin to believe your own superstitions—anyway I do. So then you can see yourself how it must have made me feel when Murphy called.'

'How?' I said. (Only thing I could think of.)

'Gave me a jolt,' he said.

Poor Ben looked at us and we looked at him and he turned again and looked at his watch. 'You take a horse who's had blinders on all day—before your time Toni, I know—by the time he's worked all day and you unharness him in the evening he's used to that narrow vision, and if he's a young horse it may be he'll jump forty feet from a finger raised off to the side where he'd forgot anything could be; once in a while one will, specially if he hasn't been out many times in blinders: that's why I said a young horse, but I've been out a few times and I'm not so young,' and he laughed.

'Not a horse either, I hope,' I said. He'd laid around

94

alone so long and thought so much and got so excited that he could hardly make sense. But I could see they liked it. I was afraid he'd start up again, but after he lay there smiling a minute he rolled his head and looked at his watch and told us he guessed he'd have to let us leave.

Later on when we were alone I asked Margaret: 'You like Ben all right?'

'Yes, he seems nice. Do you like him?'

'Sure.'

'You looked a little glum in there.'

'Didn't know anyone was looking. Just a passing fancy,' I said. 'He's a good man. I told you a long time ago, nothing the matter with him—just physical ailments and debts.'

'Does he seem very changed?'

'Chattered more. He always did have a social streak though. A lot of these old loners do. Once or twice a month they'll stop you and talk your head off. Gives them something to brood about afterwards. But I never heard him go on about himself quite like he did tonight. Probably afraid after we'd had a look at him we'd skip town and he'd never see her again.'

'He may really have felt something almost like that,' Margaret said.

'I'll tell you what,' I said, 'if it looks like they're about to get tapped off all right together, let's leave town for a few days, just you and me.'

'Good idea,' she said.

The next morning I got up and went over to the café early. I'd told the women the night before that if they wanted to see the men of the soil all gathered together they'd have to get up in the morning. The café's crowded till about six, thins out after. Toni said she thought she'd

95

sleep. Margaret said she'd get up, but when morning came and she looked out and couldn't see anything, she wouldn't get out of bed.

There were thirty or forty men in the place. I said hello to a few, saw Roy up at the counter. 'Margaret may come over in a bit,' I said, and we moved to a table. 'Fine woman, I'll say,' he said, 'both of them.'

'Sure are,' I said.

'Did you find Ben in good spirits?'

'Spirits seemed good, flesh wasn't much,' I said.

'I'll bet he was glad to see you folks.'

'He was. He was glad and so was she. Looks like something may hatch there, Roy, between him and my niece. Little early to be saying so, but just between you and me. Nothing the matter with him beyond what a person can see, I hope?'

'I'll say not,' Roy said. 'He's never drank anymore after that one session.'

'The wife ever heard from?'

'Never came back. They got a divorce, sure did. Clean that way.'

'And does he have to pay on that? Not that it's any of my business. But I feel kind of obliged to look out for her, doesn't have many relations who take an interest.'

'Well, I don't know as I should say, but he doesn't pay a penny out of that kind, no, sure doesn't. The first wife died, so that's all well; and with the middle one, he had a daughter by her and had to pay some on that, but she's her own person now, the daughter is. You know this last wife was his third.'

'That's all to the good then,' I said, 'but I guess he's so far in debt to the hospital and doctors that it's foolish even to inquire about his other debts?'

'No, he's got hardly a debt in the world, Murphy. He never could touch the banks for much.'

'That's what I say: that medical bill dwarfs all.'

'No, that was covered.'

'Well, well. How so? If you don't mind my asking.'

'Well, you know he's worked one day a week for old Jim Evans down at the auctionyard for years and done quite a bit of stockhauling for him besides. . . .' And Roy gave me a long explanation about how Jim Evans with the help of Ben's wife had managed ten years ago to get him on a medical plan—against Ben's will since he had to sign his name two or three times and pretend to read through some papers.

'That's good to hear,' I said. 'If you don't mind my asking, Roy, is there anything at all the matter with the man besides what's visible?—it won't go beyond here.'

'I wouldn't say so, Murphy,' he said; don't know what he meant by it—'Say, here's an old buddy of yours.'

It was Gordon. I shook his hand—just as big as it ever was, and after he'd sat down and had a chance to order I said to him: 'Gordon, Roy and I were just sitting here talking about Ben behind his back. Seems I may have to have him as a nephew.'

'I heard something about that.'

'Doesn't surprise me, since we've been here over-night. Well, you'll understand then, I'm reviewing the man's qualities. May be a little premature, but I'd like to give him a clean bill of health so I can relax and enjoy the rest of my vacation. On the other hand, I'd kick myself if anything slipped by for lack of endeavor. So far I can't seem to find any hidden vices in him or even much in the way of debts. Now if you were going to list the man's faults and knew it wouldn't go any farther than this table, what would you say they are?'

'I don't care where they go and there's just one—bad luck.'

'Bad luck; well, that's a bad one. What do you think of that, Roy?' I said.

'Kind of a hard-luck man in the past all right—and felt it, too, was the worst thing,' Roy said. 'Maybe now he's a new man, though, like he says himself.'

'I don't know what else you can judge by but the past,' Gordon said.

'But the man does seem to be in high spirits, Gordon,' I said.

'Won't last,' he said, and looked at me like he thought I'd lost my understanding.

'Probably not, but they do seem to have done a complete remodeling job on that stomach, and Roy tells me it's all paid for, and now this woman's showed up—nice young woman just when he could use one. Could it be his luck's changed?'

'Never happens,' Gordon said. 'I haven't seen many good-luck women in my day, either—none up close; nothing against yours.'

'Here's someone you know coming,' Roy said to me.

'Sit down,' I said. 'Gordon, I'd like you to meet my wife, Margaret, and this is Margaret's niece, Toni Wilson. Ben has medical insurance, turns out.'

'Good. Is that what you dreamt about all night, Ben's bills?' Margaret said. 'Oh, my it's early, can I have a sip of your coffee?'

'Take one,' I said.

'We're the only women eating in here,' Toni said.

'Best-looking ones, too,' I said. 'We've just been talking

privately about Ben, and Gordon said he wishes him well but he's afraid he's been a hard-luck Ben from the word go. And I said, "Well, they have rebuilt his stomach and the bill's all paid, so it appears maybe his luck has changed." But Gordon just looked at me as if to say, "Murphy, any hard-luck man has to have his hopes tickled now and again, that's what makes it so hard." Unless I misinterpreted your look?' Gordon shrugged and gave me another look just like the first. 'But Roy's opinion seems to be that a change in luck is possible and may even have taken place. But it's hard to say whether Roy believes it himself or's just sympathizing with Ben's own opinion—and Ben's opinion I wouldn't say is worth much in a case like this.'

'It is, it's hard to say, sure is,' Roy said.

'Now you women have seen him and know a little about him, so we've elected to ask your opinion before it's too late, for what it's worth.'

'It's five-thirty in the morning,' Toni said.

'Are those pancakes good? I want to decide what to order first,' Margaret said.

'They look good,' Toni said.

'Here,' I said, and pushed my plate over in front of the two of them.

Gordon rolled his eyes and looked down his nose, and if he'd got up and left I wouldn't have been surprised. He had a wife of his own south of town, but he didn't let her eat from his plate (and from what I'd heard she had no urgent desire to).

'Now what's all this about Ben?' Margaret said.

'Is he a new man or not?' I said.

'How should I know? He seems very nice.'

'So much for you. How about you?'

She grinned. 'Ask me later. But I agree with Margaret, he seems very nice.'

'Hard to say, I'll say,' Roy said, 'sure is.'

Gordon just sat.

I'd be glad enough to be seen around with even one passable woman, and two's twice as good, but they will kill a conversation.

Toni went back in to see him that night—and the next afternoon and night; and the day after that Margaret said, 'Ben will be home tomorrow.'

'All right, let's give them some air. I could use some myself,' I said. And when we were driving along on our way north again, I told Margaret: 'Well, if it jells, fine, and if it doesn't it won't break my heart, either. She'd bite her arm off for him, the way she feels right now. He's a romantic figure, laid up in bed, even if when I'm looking at him myself I can't see it. And I can see you're fond of him yourself. I only hope it's the right thing.'

'I think it is,' Margaret said.

'Then blessings upon them,' I said. 'The next main thing is to see that they settle in Pearblossom.'

'Do you think Ben will want to keep living in Wagontire?'

'So many twists in him I'd hate to try to guess. No reason for him to. She has her business in Pearblossom and he's got nothing to speak of up here—rents that little old farm and never lost any love over it that I could see. And whatever he is he's not mean-spirited, so it's hard to see what would keep him from moving. But he has a reputation for stepping on his own toes when it hurts the most. You know as much about him as I do.'

'Well, I don't know much,' she said.

'There—you see!—you don't know and you're usually right. Best not to even think about it.'

We were gone two weeks—went clear up into Idaho.

We came back into town around nine at night and took a room in the motel. Manager said Toni still had a room; we knocked; she wasn't there; so Margaret called Ben's. She was there, and told Margaret she'd be back to the motel sometime before morning for the sake of appearances.

'What's *she* care about appearances?' I said.

'I don't know. Odd, isn't it,' Margaret said.

'Means she's planning to stay and live here,' I said.

* * *

'How's it going?' I asked her in the morning (we were sitting in the café, the three of us).

'Good,' she said and held up her hand and crossed and uncrossed her first two fingers and rubbed them together —did it without thinking and then turned red as a beet.

'Good,' I said. 'You look good, too. But I never knew you to waste money on appearances so far from home. How come you're still paying rent on that motel room?'

'Well, I like to be independent,' she said.

'So you get up out of bed and drive back over here before daylight every morning? I know you better than that.'

'All right,' she said, 'I wasn't going to tell you this until later. I hope it doesn't bother you. If it weren't for the two of you I wouldn't care at all myself, in fact I think I'd kind of like it, I guess I kind of do anyway, actually—but we're not married yet, you know, so we thought we shouldn't offend anyone—around here I mean. You see'

—she leaned across the table—'we'll be living here. It's not just that, either—' she took hold of our wrists and looked around like she was plotting a robbery and whispered, 'Don't tell anyone, but Ben's taking over the lease on this café.'

I gave Margaret a 'you see!' look. 'What's he want with a café?' I said. 'Worked outdoors all his life.'

'He says that's why,' Toni said, and laughed—breaking our hearts and couldn't keep from laughing; irritated me.

'And you? What you going to do?'

'Train horses.'

'What kind of foolishness is that? These Wagontire farmers won't pay money to have their horses trained—even by a curiosity like you.'

'I know, but in Klamath Falls I could do all right. There's an indoor arena there at the fairgrounds that I could use in the winter. I already talked to them.'

'Already huh? My, my.' I'd been about to bring up winter myself. 'You know there's cafés in Pearblossom?'

'Ben likes this one,' she said, 'and I guess I do too.'

'Does a fair business,' I said (had to say it, since the place was full of people at that moment and had been almost every time we'd been in). 'Well, I'm at a loss. You might as well have told me you'd decided to enter a convent. Café's the last thing Ben has an aptitude for, if you want my honest opinion.'

She stopped smiling and looked down—didn't want my honest opinion. 'You know why he wants a café?' I asked her.

She looked at me and shrugged.

'I don't either,' I said. 'He used to sit in here and drink milk and eat toast while the rest of us drank coffee and ate. Didn't appear to be in agony at the time, but maybe that's at the bottom of it: wants his revenge.'

'Is that a joke?' Margaret said.

Toni looked at me without smiling.

'What's he going to do in here himself?' I said. 'Over-see?'

'That and cook,' Toni said and gave me such a straight, steady bold look, and looked so solemn, that I saw it wasn't Ben who was going to be judged here and now, or maybe anytime from now on, but me. So I ran up the white flag—had to.

'Took me by surprise,' I said, 'but what do I know about it?—maybe he'll make a go of it.'

'Anyway, I'm sorry if it makes you feel bad,' she said. 'I really am.'

I understood by that that she really was, and that she was also impatient and didn't much like being made to feel bad herself.

'Aw, don't you be sorry,' I said.

When we saw her at noon she let fall another bit of news: she'd decided to stay on in Wagontire for a few weeks; then she'd come back to Pearblossom by herself or with Ben, wind things up and move.

'How long you going to pay rent on the motel room?' I said.

'Seems like a waste, doesn't it,' she said and laughed, but never answered the question. Crossed my mind they were just waiting for us to leave town (which we were doing day after next), and then they'd marry. But like most things that cross a person's mind, it turned out not to be so.

She and Margaret spent the afternoon in Klamath Falls shopping.

'Toni buy much?' I asked Margaret that night, thinking

she might have bought something that would give her plans away.

'A pair of moccasins.'

Couldn't make much out of that.

'Toni said she and Ben want us to come over to Ben's for supper tomorrow tonight,' Margaret said.

'All right. I'd as soon eat off him as anyone,' I said. 'Going to cook, is he?'

'Yes.'

'She say what their marrying plans are?'

'No, she didn't say, and I think she wanted me not to ask.'

'Sounds about right,' I said. 'I don't see what she wants to be so coy for. . . . Margaret, I've been thinking it over.'

'Thinking what over?'

'Just out of curiosity I stopped by the auctionyard this afternoon and asked old Jim Evans what kind of a man Ben is.'

'What did he say?'

'I asked him what Ben knew about the workings of the business. He said there was nothing wrong with Ben, but he's just done flunkey work for him—following cows up and down the alleys and closing the gates behind them, nothing a monkey couldn't be taught to do except they'd have you in jail for it. That's what he said, but anyhow then he said Ben was the best man he ever had for working sick. I told him: "That won't help him much now, Jim —seems to be in fine health." "Well, he'll work well, too," he said, "sick or well either one, and in the winter too, nothing wrong with him." That's about all I could get out of him.'

'Probably all there was,' Margaret said.

'Is she dying to move up here and live, do you think?'
I said. 'For herself?'

'I don't think it's a big issue one way or the other, for
her,' Margaret said.

'You think it would be wrong of me to stick my nose
into it? Delicately, I mean?'

'Not necessarily. Ben might, though,' she said. 'Why?'

'Crossed my mind to offer him a job—down there in
my auctionyard.'

'Would he take one?'

'Naw,' I said. 'That's why a man like him works for
everyone in the world—day here and a day there—hauling cattle for every farmer in the country and riding for
these different ranches, and sixteen hours a day all summer farming for himself. Makes him imagine he's independent. They hate like the devil to work for a boss.
Partnership's the only thing that might interest him.'

'You'd offer him a partnership in the auctionyard?'
(First time I ever surprised her.)

'Not if I had any sense I wouldn't.'

'But that's what you're thinking of?'

'Anyway have to pretend to.'

'Pretend to? How?'

'Couldn't; you're right. Couldn't just pretend to. Don't
you think I know that? Have to be the real thing. Have
to lie my head off, too—to make him believe I can't get
along without a valuable experienced man like him—
since he hasn't got a nickel.'

'But would the two of you be able to get along?'

'Get along together? Best not to think about it,' I said.

'Well, I like the idea,' she said.

'Doesn't surprise me,' I said. I looked at her to try to

see what she liked best about it—Toni or Ben. Naturally no telling.

The next day, about the middle of the morning—last day we'd be in Wagontire—I went out and bought some papers—gone an hour or so. When I came back I handed a newspaper to Margaret, sat down and started to read. After a few minutes I said to her:

'I'm going to drive over to Ben's at noon and prime him a little. Then tonight I'll say something nice about his cooking, and pitch it to him.'

'The partnership? Ben and Toni have gone to town,' she said.

'What do you mean?—you can see the whole town from here,' I said.

'I don't know, that's what they both told me on the phone,' she said. 'Maybe they meant a different town.'

'Not likely,' I said. 'If Ben said "town"—around here when they say "town" they mean Wagontire—unless he was trying to pull some kind of a fast one and told you a fib. You remember exactly how he put it?'

'I called to talk to Toni, and Ben said she was out in the field on a horse, so I said I'd call back, and he said he'd better have her call me, because as soon as she came in they intended to go to town.'

'Well, maybe they haven't left yet,' I said.

'When Toni called back she said they were about to get in the car, and that was half an hour ago. She said she was just going to change her shirt and leave.'

'Don't need to change your shirt to come to Wagontire,' I said. 'Gone to Reno, what'll you bet?'

'What a conclusion to jump to!'

'Don't see what else it could be. Just like him, to drag her off down there alone and marry her in private behind

106

our backs. Not that they don't have a perfect right to do however they please.'

'They certainly have,' she said.

'No law says I have to like it, though. I know how to find out, too—' and I picked up the phone and called down to Gordon's, which was ten or twelve miles south of Ben's on the highway to Reno. Gordon's wife answered and I asked her if she could ask Ben, if he happened to stop by on his way south, if he could pick me up a box of good cigars in Reno—didn't have any to amount to anything at the store in Wagontire and we had some friends who were getting married. She said she sure would be glad to —could even have gone out and flagged Ben down for me (they heard every car from the time it topped the grade where the tracks crossed the road two miles north; gave them plenty of time to get out and see who it was), but it was too late, she said: 'They went by ten or fifteen minutes back. Who's getting married?' 'Sorry, but it's a secret,' I said.

'Well, I was right,' I said to Margaret. 'Perverse trick, after all the trouble we've gone to over them. Could at least have waited till we were out of town. I'd have loaned her the money for one more night's room rent.'

'Don't be silly,' Margaret said, 'they must have decided to do it today so we could help them celebrate before we leave.'

'Big of them,' I said. 'I've half a notion to let him have his heart's desire in that café and see how it suits him. Serve him right and her too. You know he already drove one wife off trying to keep her here in this climate when she wasn't used to it.'

'But maybe Toni wants to try living here herself,' Margaret said.

'What's she know what she wants?' I said. 'I wouldn't ship an ox from that climate to this one if it was me—shows a lack of respect.'

'You'd better go out for a walk,' Margaret said.

That night when we went to supper I had a little surprise of my own ready in my coat pocket, just to show them they couldn't get away with anything, or not as much as they thought they could. Even Margaret didn't know about it.

They met us at the door. 'You two look bright,' I said. Ben had on a white shirt—looked like it just came off the cardboard that morning—and had gone so far as to tie a red silk scarf around his neck. He'd just shaved; his mop of hair was combed back flat, still damp from the shower so it hadn't bushed up yet—first time I ever saw the shape of his whole big bony head—rawboned fellow for sure. But he was in good flesh, had almost a bloomy look, pink cheeked; only, on his neck under the scarf the skin had prickled up and turned red.

Toni was flushed from the heat of the kitchen and maybe a little excited, but calm. She'd laugh at you and look right at you while she did it. Had on her new moccasins, otherwide dressed just like always—pair of jeans and a solid-colored long-sleeved shirt—neat as a pin. She didn't look young but she looked young enough to be his daughter.

'Come into the kitchen,' Ben said, 'I'm going to make you compliment me on my housecleaning job.'

'Let me throw this coat down somewhere,' I said.

'Here, I'll take it, Murphy,' Ben said, and reached out, but I wouldn't let him have it.

'Just tell me where to put it,' I said. 'I always like to hang my coat up myself, so if I have to make a run for it I know where it is.'

He laughed. 'Well, hang it right up here by the door then with mine,' he said.

'My, there has been a change in this kitchen,' Margaret said.

'Scrubbed down, walls and all,' I said. 'Couldn't see the soot on the ceiling for the cobwebs before. Did you get any work out of Toni?'

'He had it done before he'd even let me see it,' Toni said.

'Always curious to see how far an old dyed-in-the-wool bachelor will go,' I said. 'I never knew you could cook, either.'

'Hasn't been proved yet,' Ben said, and winked. 'I used to cook a fair amount. Lost the habit living alone.'

'Lamb smells good,' I said. 'I've always liked lamb—as a meat dish.'

'I lost a considerable sum of money on a band of sheep once,' Ben said. 'Got so I kind of liked them time I was done, though.'

'He's in a good mood,' I thought to myself. 'They say a person gets used to everything but bad weather,' I said.

No one answered, so I answered myself: 'True in my case. I was born here and stayed better than half a century—never did get used to it.'

'I don't mind weather, long as it's on the other side of a pane or two of glass,' Ben said. 'Sort of like to look out at it.'

'Had about enough of that hard outdoor work, have you, Ben?'

'Had enough, you said it!' he said.

Toni sat us down in the front room and then ran back in the kitchen with Ben.

He'd cleared his bridles and old shirts out of the way off the furniture and moved his piles of bills and old magazines off the table, which they'd set for supper: four plates on it and no two alike. I whispered in Margaret's ear: 'Last wife cleaned him out—dishes, sheets, new bedroom set—the works. Rented a one-way trailer and old Ben loaded it up himself.'

'Who did what?' Toni said, coming in.

'Just talking about one of Ben's former wives,' I said.

'Former?' she said. 'I'm jealous. Which one?'

'Last one. Don't think I ever saw Ben wear a scarf before,' I said. 'Be a necktie next, then a yoke. Get your neck in it, too. Never know what people will do next.'

She laughed. 'What are you getting at, Murphy?'

'Not a thing,' I said, 'but I'll tell you what: it's hard to put anything over on us old fellers.'

'What do you mean?'

'Mean what I say.'

Ben came in. Toni made him lean over and whispered in his ear loud enough to hear all over the house: 'I think we'd better hurry and tell them.'

'Oh?' and he looked at her and at me and Margaret. But I wouldn't give him a sign. 'Murphy sniffing the breeze, is he?'

She nodded.

'You look like you shaved twice over today,' I said. 'Reminds me, I still have that electric razor you gave me years ago—works fine.'

'That's good,' he said. 'Daughter to one of my wives gave me that,' rubbed his big red chin and winked at Toni. 'I did shave twice, first time seems like yesterday already. Big day for us today.'

I'd hate to have to list every time he winked, but he winked again.

'Was it?' I said. 'Wasn't a very big day for us. Back and

forth between the motel and the café. I intended to run out here at noon and talk to you about a scheme of mine, Ben, but Margaret said you'd gone to town. Looked for you in town; never saw you.'

'We went for a drive south,' Ben said, and winked. I bore with it like a gentleman. 'Do you two like champagne?' Ben said. 'We're going to make you hold a glass-ful whether you do or not.'

'Playing directly into my hands,' I thought.

'I do,' Margaret said.

'I do too,' I said. 'Nice idea. Do they drink champagne as a regular thing around here now? Used to reserve it mostly for weddings, back in my day.'

'Still the same Murphy,' Ben said, 'reserve it mostly for weddings,' and winked, this time at me, as if to say he and I were the two cleverest people in the world, though maybe with just a shade of difference between us.

'Thought that's how it was,' I said. 'Ha!'—and stepped over to where my coat was hanging, pulled a bottle out of the pocket and turned around holding it up: champagne—same brand as his. 'Hard to put anything over on us old fellers, wha'd I tell you? Thought you'd managed to sneak off!'

'Guess you outfoxed us, Murphy,' Ben said—tried to sound good-natured.

'They did manage,' Margaret said, which seemed to mean, 'Sit down.'

'How did you know where we went?' Toni said. She was the only one who took it well.

'Doesn't matter,' I said, put my bottle down by theirs and sat down. 'Gordon's wife saw you go by.' Then I jumped up again and took a fresh start. 'I want to con-gratulate you both,' I said, and shook Ben's hand.

He smiled; seemed already to have forgot I'd just got the better of him.

I kissed the bride and Ben kissed Margaret; Margaret kissed Toni and then we made Ben and Toni kiss each other. Ben uncorked a bottle, and Toni brought in the champagne glasses (bought that same day) and Ben filled them.

'Ben and Toni, here's to you,' I said.

'Here's to us,' Ben said, 'and here's to us all.' We drank.

'Good antifreeze,' Ben said.

'You bet,' I said. 'Here's to marriage. I've been married my whole life long and never was done any harm by it directly, that I can remember.'

'More than I can say,' Ben said.

'Me too,' Toni said, 'but I'll drink to it.'

'Well, I will too,' Ben said.

'Smartest decision you ever made, both of you,' I said.

'Don't know if it's proper at my age,' Ben said, 'but if you and Margaret could do it we guessed we could too.'

'I've been telling Toni for years to settle down,' I said.

'He sure has,' she said. 'Is this all you meant?'

'Easy as eating a sandwich,' I said. 'Like to keep her in Pearblossom, Ben. Nice town. You ever spend any time there?'

'Never have,' he said.

'Several trees there someone planted; desert raises up and almost makes a hill. Pretty little place—best weather in the world. Biggest asset is the money that drifts out there from Los Angeles.'

'Sounds all right,' he said, without sounding terrifically excited, and pulled out his watch. 'Before I run to take care of my cooking I'd like to make one more toast,' he said.

'Good,' Toni said and leaned forward with her mouth a little open, eyes shining. They were sitting on the couch. He laughed and put his arm around her and she leaned over against him. 'Had it on my mind,' he said, 'don't know how to put it—rehearsed it so many times— but you folks know better than I do how much I have to be grateful to you for. Not much goodwill in this world, I've found—I know I've doled out little enough myself— except this kind here'—he held up the bottle—'but even it won't do the job without some of the real thing to work on.' He filled our glasses. 'Like it, don't you?' he said to Toni and cocked his head and looked down on her like he'd just bought his little girl her first soda pop. He was in a hurry to go cook except when he was talking himself —lots of time then.

'I like it,' she said.

'So I want you to know I feel a debt of gratitude— Margaret, Murphy—and here's to that.'

'Here's to it,' I said. 'I'll take all the credit I can get for it,' and we held up our glasses. 'From the time she brought your name up in a conversation and said she liked the way you killed flies, I was for it, and Margaret the minute she laid eyes on you took a shine of her own to you.'

'That's so,' Margaret said.

Toni nodded, and he turned and kissed her on the lips. 'What they won't put up with,' I said to myself. Then he walked into the kitchen. 'In an expansive mood for him,' I thought. 'Got no yen to move to Pearblossom; and that debt of gratitude is liable to do me more harm than good. On the other hand, he'll have to be a bigger fool than I think he is to turn down half an auctionyard. "Ben," I'll say to him, "now don't you deny it: you're a valuable man: don't see how I got along so well without you all these years. Anyhow, so here's what I want to propose—" '

'What?' I said.

'I said you look like you're thinking deep thoughts,' Toni said.

'Must have been, because I didn't hear you. I was thinking about Ben himself.'

'That's nice.'

'May be, but no one's going to take your word for it.'

'Why not?'

'Because you signed on the line.'

Ben came in from the kitchen.

'Ben, I was just telling her she's not a trustworthy judge of your character. Not that anything's wrong with you; but being a married woman now, if there was she'd look at it with a blind eye.'

He kissed her on top of the head. 'I sure hope so,' he said.

'I noticed when you bent over just now, haven't you let your belt out a couple of notches? You look like you've put on fifteen pounds since we saw you in the hospital.'

'Not far from it,' he said. 'Closer to ten.'

'That's quite a trick, thin as you've been for so many years.'

'Nice one,' Toni said and nodded. 'She's pink as pink, and about half giddy,' I thought. 'Doesn't seem right at her age.'

'Hope you don't start to grow,' I said. 'Don't want to draw too close a comparison, but I remember years ago —you listen to this too, Toni, since you think you know something about cattle. There was a—'

'More than you!' she said, and grinned.

'All right—then you know how tough some of those

cattle they bring up out of old Mexico are. Well—'

'I know!' she said.

Ben sat down beside her and put his hand on her thigh —a fresh wave of color ran from the roots of her hair down to her collarbone, probably farther. She leaned over against him.

'Go ahead, Murphy, I'll try to keep her under control,' he said.

'Anyhow,' I said, 'tragic thing to relate, but one summer they shipped this train-car-load of steers in here to Wagontire, straight from some Ocotillo flat down in old Mexico. Came off the train looking like greyhounds, but I don't imagine they looked much different when they left home. Never had their bellies full their whole lives long. Biggest of them no taller than a half-grown calf— but old: horns long as my arm on some of them; wonder they could hold their own heads up, little old weak things. And you couldn't have put together a good mouthful of teeth out of the bunch. Beside the point, but that load of cattle gifted us with these Mexican stickers —see them everywhere, look like sunflowers—only imported thing I ever saw that thrives here, unless it's brought from Siberia or somewhere.'

'Well, I won't bless them for bringing in those stickers, if that's their claim to fame,' Ben said, and reached to pull out his watch, but restrained himself.

'Is that what's tragic?' Toni said.

'So the man that bought them put them in a sidehill lot and dumped a truckload of cull potatoes in with them. Took them a while to take to those potatoes—never seen anything like that before; and they all but died of thirst before they'd brave that metal watertrough. They'd smell the water, tiptoe up till they'd touch that spring steel and turn and run to the far side of the pen and stand there an hour before they'd start sneaking up on it again. But before much of the summer went by they'd eat and drink just like anybody, and it didn't surprise us to see them start to get fat. But we did a doubletake when it began to look to some of us like they were starting to grow—taller I mean. At first we'd argue about it. Everyone agreed they were too old to grow, but some said they were growing anyway, some said they couldn't see it, some said it looked like it all right, but that it was a kind of optical illusion caused by their getting fat and healthy and being on a sidehill where it was hard to get a square look at them.

'But after a month had gone by, and you could see them scratch their backs and leave the hair hanging on the top wire of the fence, we were believers. Always had a lot of respect for the little monkeys after that. Lived to old age on nothing at all, waiting for something to eat with no hope of getting it, wore their teeth down to the gums processing that Mexican sand for what they could get out of it—and then when they did get something to eat, went right on and grew like calves.'

'I've seen that happen myself to some of those kind of cattle,' Ben said. 'That's interesting, though.'

'I don't see what's tragic about it,' Margaret said.

'This here,' I said. 'Winter came, snow flew and *Dear John*—that's all she wrote: kiss of death to them.'

'Really?' Margaret said.

'Just lived a few days. Cross my heart. Time enough to gather their thoughts. Pneumonia. Ask Ben—he knows this climate.'

'Used to happen once in a while before we got antibiotics. Better get you a flu shot,' he said to Toni, and they both laughed.

'There's a lesson in it just the same,' I said. 'Ben, Margaret said the best way to approach you is straight on, being a straightforward man yourself. You say you owe me a debt of some kind. Well, you don't owe me a thing. But let me put it to you this way.' He pulled out his watch. 'You know I'm in the auctionyard business now, and I—'

'Hold off just one minute, Murphy, and we'll go at it over supper.'

'You won't regret it,' I said. 'No hurry.'

Toni and Ben put the food on the table. I saw she carried herself just fine, a pitcher of gravy in one hand and a bowl of peas in the other. I'd hoped she was drunk.

We sat down and started to eat. I kept quiet at first: thought Ben would pick up the subject again himself, if just out of politeness, hoped he might, but no.

'It's good,' Margaret said.

'Sure is,' I said, 'shouldn't surprise anyone. Person can do one thing, he can generally do another. You've been working at the auctionyard here in Wagontire for some years now, Ben. Know the business.'

'I know the sorriest end of it pretty well,' he said.

'If you don't mind my saying so, you're a valuable man there just the same. Old Jim told me so himself. I went by on purpose to ask him, to tell the truth.'

'We made a deal—I don't do much and he doesn't pay me much,' Ben said, and laughed, which made Toni laugh with her mouth full; sputtered, shook her head and her eyes watered, and then she had to laugh at that.

'Little idiot,' I thought.

But Ben smiled down on her like she'd just borne him twins. All eyes where she was concerned. Made it a little

117

hard to engage his interest in anything else—or I hoped that was all the problem.

'Ben, to be brief, here's what I have in mind,' I said. 'I have that auctionyard—sell mostly horses.' He'd been watching her chew, but he turned and looked at me in a friendly way.

'Doing all right, is it?' he said.

'Makes more money than I know how to spend,' I said.

'Glad to hear it. We all said you'd land on your feet down there if anyone would. Margaret, let me slice you off another little bit of meat—which side do you like it from?'

'Either one, thank you,' she said.

'Murphy, how about you?'

'Over there where it's brownest. Thanks. I—'

'Mrs.?' he said to Toni. So I waited. She didn't want any, but they had to mingle looks; baby could have been born of those looks, but I preferred them to the winks.

'I like it better than I did the store,' I said. 'Get outside and around. Talk to people if I feel like it, if I don't I won't.'

'When did you ever not feel like talking to anyone?' Toni said.

'A person like me'll talk to anyone comes along, you're right,' I said, 'but a person like Ben—you know yourself best, Ben, but it's hard to picture you behind the counter in a café, giving the time of day to every clodkicker who takes it into his head to come in—I mean people you stopped nodding to on the street years back. The business I'm in down there, I'm not beholden to anybody and don't have to pretend to be.'

'I might nod to most anybody, the way I feel right now,' Ben said.

'You're in the first flush of new love, if you don't mind my saying so.'

'No, I don't mind,' he said, and turned and beamed down on her till I was sorry I mentioned it.

'Good condition to be in,' I said, 'but I wouldn't try to draw conclusions from it. Six months from now when old Sterling Green tracks muddy snow in the door of that café and nudges you with his elbow and signs the ticket for his hamburger and lays down a nickel tip, you won't put up with him any better than you used to.'

'Now there's a picture,' Ben said, and laughed aloud. 'I'll turn him out, sure enough, but I won't lose any sleep over it tonight.' And he winked at Toni.

'So I like the auction business,' I said. 'I'm independent, I get out and around—only not out where I can't get back in should the weather suggest it (no weather down there to speak of anyway). Usually drive out in the countryside in the morning, look over a few animals. Never get far from the coffeepot. Couldn't call it work; and I make money.' I saw I had his attention. 'Hold one sale a week— Friday nights—figure that's best, seeing as it's payday for a lot of people. Sale runs darned near all night sometimes. Don't know what would happen if we'd advertise. Should hold two sales a week, even now. But lazy as I've got, and there by myself, I won't bother—turn business away as it is. Wouldn't think those commissions would add up like they do—little old six percent, but—'

'Murphy, I—'

'Commission here, commission there,' I said, 'adds up. Man'll come up from L.A., say, buy a horse, change his mind a week later—nothing the matter with the horse, but now he wants a boat instead, or his wife has left him or his daughter grew up while he wasn't looking. I've seen the same old horse go through the sales ring a dozen times in a year and nothing the matter with him—commission every time. Now, you multiply that by—'

'Murphy,' he said, 'I'm going to turn you down.'

'Haven't made you an offer yet,' I said. 'Was going to, though—full half interest.' I looked at his eyes when I said 'full half interest': never a spark.

'I sure hate to be in the position of having to turn you down,' he said, 'but there it is. All these latter years I've had a daydream of being in out of the weather—and now I've got it connected up with this café here in Wagontire. May be foolish, but my heart's set on it. Unless Toni was adverse to the idea, and from the talks we've had I don't honestly think she is.'

They gave each other another one of those big looks.

'You don't know what she wants anymore than she knows herself,' I thought. 'You've swept her off her feet, Ben, damn your obstinate soul.' 'Ben, that's all right,' I said. 'You know your own mind. Disappoints me, but don't feel you owe me a thing. Café might not be the same in reality, though.'

He laid his fork down and sat up straight. 'Same as what?' he said, and raised his chin and fixed me with his eyes. Margaret nudged me under the table.

'Same as you imagine,' I said.

Toni looked from Ben to me and back.

'Not that it's any of my business,' I said.

'No,' he said, and started tapping the table with his fingertips, lips pressed flat and that big red jaw set.

'Missus might not thrive here either, Ben,' I said, 'whatever she may think herself. Lot of them haven't— imported women, I mean—as you know yourself from experience. Hate to mention it.'

'Murphy, stop it,' Toni said. 'That's enough.'

'You women if you can't be agreeable keep out of it,' I said.

Poor Ben resembled a madman. His eyes were bugged and seemed to come at me separately, from two directions. Exercised a lot of restraint, I'll say that for him. I believe if he'd flown at me with the one hand (the one on the table), at the same time he'd have grabbed his own neck and choked himself with the other. He pushed his chair back and stood up—looked tall as a tree from where I sat, and I thought for sure he'd mar his wedding night by violence. But he turned and walked fast into the kitchen, his back swelled up to half again its natural size.

The back door banged.

'Damn—Ben went out so fast without excusing himself I didn't get to praise his supper. We made a dent in him,' I said, nodding at the remains of the leg of lamb.

Toni jumped up and went through the kitchen and out the door—didn't say a word, either.

'You're causing trouble,' Margaret said (seemed to be the only one who'd talk to me).

'So hard to get Ben's attention, thought I might as well say something once I had it.'

'Why do you goad him so?'

'Felt like it,' I said. She didn't say anything.

Toni came back in in a minute and sat down.

'Where's old Ben off to?' I said.

She mumbled something and wouldn't look at me.

'What?' I said.

'Irrigating!' she said, louder than she needed to.

'Wish he'd mentioned it, I'd have helped him,' I said. 'Do him good though to get out for a bit. This Wagontire air will cool a person off fast.'

'Murphy, I'm furious at you,' Toni said, and looked at me solemn as a judge out of those dark eyes.

'You've never been furious in your life,' I said.

She turned a little red. 'I do want to stay here and live,' she said.

'No reason not to,' I said, 'just the weather. You'll make as good friends here as anywhere. You have to say you want to whether you do or not; doesn't matter much what you say, now you're married. I told you that already.'

'Ben would be very willing to move. He's said so.'

'Has? I didn't hear him.'

'No, you didn't hear him, but he has.'

'He's the one turned down the deal—we all three sat here and heard that.'

'I asked him to.'

'That right? When was that? I never heard you.'

'A few days ago.'

'I didn't make you an offer days ago.'

'I thought you might make one.'

'You trying to tell me you turned me down.'

'As much as anyone else did, yes.' She blushed. 'We thought it would be better if it came from Ben, but now after the way you've been acting I—'

'Well, fine then,' I said, and stood up. 'I ought to be used to it, coming from you—no problem at all—only wish I'd understood it earlier—my apologies to Ben— believe I'll get some air myself.'

I grabbed my coat and went out the front door. Walked down the lane that ran through the orchard about a quarter mile to the road, then turned and walked back. 'Damn,' I said to myself, 'thought I got used to being turned down by her years ago—damn sure ought to have.

Well, let her suffer Wagontire then and more power to her. See if she makes friends here to equal the ones she has there. Hurts though—damn—damn fool me,' kept repeating myself and mumbled out loud like a man who's stubbed his old sore toe, which I as much as had.

When I got to the house I was very little better off than when I'd left it, so I headed back up the lane for another march. Halfway to the road again, I heard a twang, then made out Ben up ahead of me, climbing through the orchard fence. He came down the lane carrying his shovel.

'Sorry, Ben,' I said when we passed in the dark, and he nodded—stiff as a rod, but he wouldn't have nodded at all if he hadn't been willing to patch it up.

He went on into the house, and I took a couple more trips up and down, when it dawned on me my feet were tired. I'd been out a good twenty minutes and I could stay out till my shoes wore out before anyone was going to come out looking for me—I could see that—so I might as well go in. Felt calmer.

I saw them lit up through the front-room window. They'd moved to the softer furniture. Ben had the coffee-pot in his hand—he was standing up—and I watched him bend over and fill Margaret's cup. Margaret said something and they all three laughed—I couldn't imagine what for. Appeared my absence hadn't made much of a dent in the proceedings. 'Just as well,' I told myself. Still, it didn't seem quite right, and I was tempted to go in and try to stir things up with an apology or two, at least.

They stopped and all looked up when I came in the door, and I decided I'd better settle for that. 'Here he is,' Ben said. Poured me some coffee and even offered to spike it. (I never saw a man try harder to behave himself.

I didn't see him glance at his watch once, the whole rest of the evening.)

'Not me, thanks, Ben,' I said. And he didn't take any brandy in his coffee himself, but Margaret and Toni each took a big shot, and a few minutes later another.

Five minutes after the second one Toni pushed back her chair and stood up—tried to: went white in the face, buckled her knees and grabbed hold of the table edge; didn't fall, but from the looks of her face the room was tipping.

We all jumped up.

'Are you all right?!' Margaret said.

'Yes,' she said, shook her head trying to clear it and kept hold of the table.

'Sit down,' I said. 'Liquor pulled a sneak on you.'

'Something did,' she said. She smiled at poor Ben, who looked worse than she did; he stared at her like he couldn't speak.

'You're all right?' he said.

'Yes, but I think I'd better lie down for a minute.' She walked into the bedroom with hardly a wobble, Ben sneaking along behind with his hand by her elbow, so full of solicitude he didn't dare reach all the way out and touch her.

We sat there, Margaret and I. Could hear Ben and Toni talking, couldn't make out the words but it sounded pretty romantic in tone.

'I'm sorry they want to stay here,' Margaret said.

'None of my business anyway,' I said.

'No,' she said.

'Quite a glitter he gets in his eyes,' I said. 'I'd like to have a photograph of it to show him sometime when he's in his right mind.'

'Shh,' she said.

After about ten minutes Ben came back in smiling to himself. 'She's asleep,' he said. 'So what?' I said to myself: you'd think she was the first drunk who ever fell asleep. 'She made me promise she'd be able to say goodnight to you folks before you leave. "Wake me up if I should happen to fall asleep," she says, and then lies down on top of the bed—' he snapped his fingers—'sound asleep!'

He said his coffee was cold and that he'd go heat up some more and that we should sit down again on the couch and keep him company and have some more coffee. 'All right,' I said, 'I'll drink one more cup myself, don't put any of those knockout drops in mine, though; then we really had better get on back over to the motel.'

While Ben was in the kitchen Margaret and I heard the springs creak several times in the bedroom. Margaret went in to see her, and came back at the same time Ben came in with the coffee. 'Toni's awake,' she said.

'Is she all right?' Ben said.

'Fine,' Margaret said. 'Sleepy, but she says she wants to visit. I'm going to sit with her a minute.'

Ben took a chair in for Margaret. Hardly a stick of furniture in that bedroom—I saw it myself ten minutes later.

So Ben and I carried on a conversation—steered clear of anything worth mentioning. 'Whatever happened to old Bob Jones who used to have the old Heaton place— you know, down there just across the road from the Chinaman's?' I asked him. 'Nothing, he's still there,' Ben said. 'I'll be darned,' I said. Till Margaret came in. She said Toni refused to go to sleep until I'd come in so she could tell me goodbye.

'Guess I can manage that,' I said. 'Right now?'

'Wait just a few minutes,' Margaret said.

We heard the bedsprings creak and lift as she got up, the floor creak, the toilet flush and the water run from the tap, the floor creak and then the bed as she lay back down—wasn't much of a bed. A few minutes passed without a sound coming out of there. I think we all half expected her to call out.

'Well, let's go in and tell the girl goodnight—probably suffering agonies trying to stay awake,' I said.

'I already did,' Margaret said.

Ben looked out the window.

I stood up. 'Ben, you show me the way.'

'All right,' he said, and led me to the door of the bedroom and stood aside for me to pass on in; but I caught him and gave him a little shove in her direction.

'Watch out you don't trip over anything in this boar's nest,' he said. Actually wasn't enough in there to trip over; I saw her suitcase open on the floor by the bed.

We stood over the bed, and I blinked trying to see. She'd left the light on in the closet, but the closet door threw a shadow across her—hard to make out her features at first. She was lying with the pillows behind her, half sitting up; I imagined I saw her looking at me— would have been natural; then I saw her eyes were closed.

'Hey, you,' Ben said, not very loud.

'Shh, that's all right,' I said. 'She's sound asleep.'

'Looks like she had her heart in the right place, Murphy—fell asleep sitting up. She'll clean my plow for me if I let you go off without saying goodnight. Hey, you— wake up. Toni! Here's Murphy,' and he touched her on the shoulder. Couldn't bring himself to do any more, and she only gave her head a tiny shake 'no' and frowned—asleep.

'Shh, that's all right,' I said. 'Leave her be.' She had one of his shirts on—fit her like a tent. It was a white shirt and she looked almost as white. She'd rolled the sleeves up. Her left arm lay by her side with the sleeve rolled just a little way up her forearm; she had her right arm folded across her belly, so you could see it rise and settle with her breath, and the sleeve had somehow drifted up over her elbow.

'Don't bother her, Ben. Isn't she a sweet thing? Sleeping like a baby. A man wants to keep care of what he has. You keep care of her,' I whispered.

Then I was afraid he might take offense, though I don't think I intended any for the moment.

'She pretty much insists on taking care of herself,' he said. 'I'll try though, Murphy.'

'One of these big cold-backed northern horses takes a notion to fall with her on that hard frozen ground here in the wintertime, she might not get up to tell the story —so you make her ride inside that indoor arena when the ground's frozen,' I said. 'You hear?'

'All right, sure will,' he said, looking down at her. 'I'll tell her, and I'll tell her you said so, too.' I believe he felt such an excess of benevolence, looking at her sleeping, that I got some of the overflow.

'You'll have to tell her again in the winter,' I said. 'You remember because she won't.'

'I'll remember,' he said. 'Anyway, we'll be in touch—you drop her a line yourself; mean a lot to her.'

Then we went out.

We thanked him for supper, and he thanked us six times over for everything. And that was the end of it.

Three weeks later Toni rode down to Pearblossom (I mean as close to here as the trains go), settled her affairs and moved to Wagontire—even talked a couple of her customers into sending their horses clear up there for her to train.

* * *

Margaret called her up again this evening. Nice cool January evening in Pearblossom, can't go out after midnight without a sweater on.

'Oh, that's fine,' Margaret said. 'Really? Well, tell Ben I said to just keep on that way.'

Wasn't worth listening to so I walked out into the other room.

'They still married?' I asked Margaret.

'Seem to be fine,' Margaret said.

'Likes riding that frozen ground, does she?'

'You know she never mentions that kind of thing to me. Maybe she uses the indoor place.'

'She say how cold it is?'

'Only that it's cold.'

'Ashamed to say. How's he like his café?'

'She says business is slow this time of year, but so far he likes it.'

'He'll starve warm, then, just like he wanted. Not eaten up by ambition, I'll say that for him. Well, that's fine. Didn't say a thing of interest, then?'

'She said to tell you she has some electric socks.'

'What's she want to tell me that for?'

'Friendliness, judging by the tone of her voice.'

I sat on in the front room. 'Slow,' I said to myself. 'Bound to be slow this time of year. Odd she'd mention it—means *he* did. Course he may like it slow. Not likely. More likely kicking himself for having turned down that auctionyard; too proud to say so directly, even to her. Well, Wagontire's a long way to travel just to look into his old long face and try to figure out what he's thinking. Specially by car. Train's not so bad. . . . No, can't do it—not now: she's stubborner than he is, that's the real trouble. Best not push them too hard, like I did last time. Better wait till March or even April—then see how she's weathered it. Hope they have a long hard winter.'